M.

Buckingham Manor

BY

DAVID DOWSON

www.daviddowson.com

www.daviddowson.co.uk

daraarts@sky.com

Acknowledgements

Special thanks to my mother, Beryl, who is always there for me and my sister, Jan Webber, author of the Betty Illustrated Children's books.

CHAPTER 8 2

All rights reserved

Edition ONE

Copyright © David Dowson 01/01/24

www.daviddowson.com

www.daviddowson.co.uk

daraarts@sky.co.uk

11/02/24

Other books also written by David Dowson include:

Chess for Beginners

Chess for Beginners Edition 2

Into the Realm of Chess Calculation

Nursery Rhymes

The Path of a Chess Amateur

CHESS: the BEGINNERS GUIDE eBook:

NOVELS

Declon Five.

Dangers within

The Murder of Inspector Hine

Spooks Scarlett's Enigma

The Deception Unveiled

Webs of Blood and Shadows

CHAPTER 8 4

CONTENTS

CHAPTER 8   5

CHAPTER1

Lakshmi stood frozen in the opulent drawing room, her heart pounding. Her hands trembled uncontrollably as she took in the scene before her. Lady Grace shot up from her seat at the sight of Lakshmi, her eyes blazing with fury and shock. She held up a vial containing white powder. "One of the servants found this in your room." Lady Grace spat. The room was filled with an eerie silence, broken only by Lakshmi's shallow breaths. Panic consumed her as she realized the situation she found herself in. "Lakshmi! What have you done?" Lady Grace's voice quivered with a mix of anguish and anger. The accusation sent shockwaves through Lakshmi's body, seizing her voice momentarily. Finally finding her words, she stammered, "My Lady, I... I didn't do anything. I just arrived a few minutes ago and heard the news that I am responsible for her death." She'd been told that Lord Michael suddenly ordered a search of all

CHAPTER 8

the rooms in the house, struck by some impulse that the murderer would be found within the walls of Buckingham mansion. Lady Grace's eyes narrowed as she scrutinized her. "How convenient. You conveniently arrived just moments before her death. You were the first person to find her lifeless body, weren't you? And now you expect me to believe you had no hand in this?" Tears welled up in Lakshmi's eyes as she pleaded her innocence. "My Lady, you must believe me. I loved Lady Michelle as my own family. I would never harm her." Just then, the door swung open, revealing Lord Michael. Panic and grief filled his eyes as he rushed towards Lakshmi, trying to hit her. "Michelle! No, please, no!" Lady Grace yelled and held him back. Lord Michael turned towards his wife, and his voice laced with suspicion. "And where were you when your mother-in-law needed you the most, and now you're stopping me from avenging her?" Lady Grace looked up, her eyes still red-rimmed from

CHAPTER 8 7

crying. "I... I was in my room; is that supposed to be an offence? I haven't been well, Michael. I can't believe it... I can't believe you're saying this to me right now. I have cried and still do. If justice is for me to let you kill her, then go ahead." The room was now engulfed in a cacophony of grief and confusion. Lakshmi's head spun with unanswered questions. Lady Michelle's death had sent shockwaves through everyone's lives but hers. It seemed like someone had set her up to be the prime suspect. She was the ideal scapegoat when no other explanation presented itself. Lord Michael's eyes burned with a fury that caused Lakshmi to flinch. He pointed a shaky finger at her. "I promise you'll receive every bit of the punishment you deserve. Guards!" Two guards marched into the room at his bellowed command, taking Lakshmi by her arms. She struggled against their tight grips. "I didn't do it, I swear!" "Lock her up until the detective arrives." Lord Michael ordered, turning his back

CHAPTER 8 8

to her. A few days passed, and Lakshmi found herself confined to her small chambers, her every move watched by the ever-present guards. Desperation clawed at her, igniting a fierce determination to prove her innocence and find the culprit responsible for Lady Michelle's demise. One evening, as the sun cast long shadows across the dimly lit hallway, Lakshmi snuck out of her room. Her heart thudded as she approached the library, hoping to find clues to the truth. As she entered the spacious room adorned with grand bookshelves and dusty tomes, she noticed a flickering candlelight behind a hidden door. Intrigued, she eased herself towards it, pushing it open gently. Surprisingly, she found herself in a hidden chamber filled with dust and forgotten secrets. As her eyes adjusted to the dim light, she gasped at the myriad documents and photographs scattered across a massive mahogany table. They were all connected to Lady Michelle; decades of her personal life laid bare before her

CHAPTER 8   9

eyes. But what caught her attention the most was a familiar face in some of the photographs: Lady Diane. Her mind spun with the implications of what she had discovered. Could Lady Diane be involved in her sister's death? And if so, why? Lost in her thoughts, she didn't notice Lord Michael's stealthy approach until it was too late. "What are you doing here, Lakshmi?" His voice, devoid of compassion, pierced through the silence. Lakshmi turned towards him, her voice steady as she held his gaze. "I came to find the truth, my Lord, to uncover who was truly responsible for Lady Michelle's death." His face was like a stone as he considered her words. He zeroed in on the picture of Lady Diane. "Do you think Lady Diane could do such a thing?" Lakshmi nodded gravely. "I don't know, my Lord, but these documents suggest there is more to Lady Michelle's demise than meets the eye. I believe someone very close to her may have orchestrated this." Lord Michael's eyes widened

CHAPTER 8 10

with disbelief and realization. "Her sister? She has always been envious of Michelle. She wanted everything that Michelle had, including her husband, but one thing she would never do was kill her sister, you twat!* Lakshmi's heart sank as she saw the pain and betrayal etched on Lord Michael's face. He didn't believe her. "I promise you, my Lord, I will uncover the truth. Lady Michelle deserves justice. "" Go back to your room." Lord Michael said, ignoring her words. " If you try to escape again, I'll be forced to hurt you." A shiver ran down her spine at his threat. She didn't know if Lord Micha would carry out his words, but the severity of the situation was beginning to dawn on her; she was being accused of murder. There was something suspicious going on in the house. Days had passed, and she had yet to be arrested for anything.

Whether she believed his threat or not, Lakshmi stayed put in her room.

The days trickled by; she spent them alone,

CHAPTER 8 11

unsure if the rest of the house had been rebuked from visiting her or if they believed she was guilty. It wasn't until a week into confinement that she was finally arrested. Lakshmi sat on the cold, hard bench inside the cramped holding cell, her heart pounding. She couldn't believe what had just happened. One moment, she'd been locked up in her room, and the next, she found herself surrounded by police officers, their stern faces glaring at her as if she were some criminal. She shook her head, trying to make sense of it all. How could this have happened? She had done nothing wrong, yet here she was, unjustly about to be confined behind the cold iron bars of the cell. Her mind was racing with questions, the most pressing being: how would she escape this dreadful predicament? As she sat there, lost in her thoughts, the back door creaked open, and a tall, burly police officer stepped inside. His bald head gleamed under the harsh fluorescent lights, and his deep voice reverberated through the

CHAPTER 8   12

empty backyard. " Ms Lakshmi, you are under arrest for the murder of Lady Michelle," the officer announced, eyeing her with an intensity that sent shivers down her spine as he held up the arrest warrant. Lakshmi's eyes widened. "I didn't kill anyone! You have it all wrong!" The officer crossed his arms, his stern expression unyielding.

"Save your protests for the court, miss. We have evidence implicating you in his murder. Eyewitnesses saw you arguing with her just hours before she was found dead, and let's not talk about the poison you used. Let's leave the explanations for the lawyers." Lakshmi's mind raced as she tried to recall the events of that day. She'd had no heated argument with Lady Michelle. She had no motive, no reason to harm her. "Officer, I admit whatever evidence you have, one might make it look like I'm responsible, but I swear, I had nothing to do with her death," Lakshmi pleaded, her voice trembling. The officer's gaze softened momentarily, but he quickly composed himself. "Innocent until proven guilty, that's how it works, Ms. Lakshmi, but you'll have to prove your innocence in court. Until then, you'll remain behind bars." Lakshmi's heart sank as the officer turned to leave, closing the cell door behind him with a rattling thud. She was alone in the cold, dreary cell, with only her thoughts and racing heartbeat. The time seemed to fly past as Lakshmi tried to piece together the puzzle of Michelle's murder. Who could have wanted Michelle dead and wanted her in prison for it? A tiny flicker of hope ignited as her mind worked through the possibilities. She had to find evidence that proved her innocence, but she couldn't do anything from behind bars. Lord Michael stumbled into the grand hall of Buckingham Manor, his face flushed and his eyes bloodshot. His steps were wobbly, but he managed to maintain an air of grandeur, even in his intoxicated state. The flickering candles cast eerie shadows against the ancient tapestries that

CHAPTER 8   14

adorned the walls as if reflecting the chaotic thoughts running through his mind. The servants watched him with cautious eyes, unsure of what mood their lord would be in tonight. Lord Michael was known to swing between bouts of fervent melancholy and wild exuberance, fueled by the countless bottles of whiskey he indulged in every evening. More often than not, the household staff found themselves on the receiving end of his drunken tirades. Tonight, however, Lord Michael's delirium seemed particularly intense. As he stumbled towards the fireplace, he bellowed, "I have summoned death into these walls! He walks amongst us, silently stealing the breath from our souls. You fools, don't you see?" The servants exchanged glances, suppressing their amusement at their lord's intoxicated ramblings. This was not the first time Lord Michael had proclaimed such a notion, and they had long learned not to take his words seriously. One of the head housekeepers approached Lord Michael cautiously, her face etched with concern. "My lord, perhaps you should retire to your chambers. You have had enough for tonight." Lord Michael scoffed, glaring at her with bloodshot eyes. "You think I'm delusional, don't you? Well, let me tell you, whatever your name is. Death has taken root in this manner. It creeps through the halls like a ghostly spectre, stealing life from the innocent." She sighed, her sage expression betraying her sympathy for the tortured soul before her. She had been serving Lord Michael for over two decades and had grown accustomed to his eccentricities. "My lord, perhaps you are mistaken. There is no evidence of any foul play within these walls."

Lord Michael turned towards the rest of the servants, his voice growing louder yet unsteady. "Don't you all see? The air grows heavy with the stench of death. It lingers in every corner, in every whispered word. I brought this plague upon us!" Silence hung in the air as the servants exchanged concerned glances. None wanted to

CHAPTER 8   16

challenge their lord's claims openly, but neither did they genuinely believe his words. They had dutifully carried out their tasks daily without any signs of supernatural occurrences in the manor. Dorothea, the head cook, finally spoke up, her voice laced with scepticism. "With all due respect, my lord, perhaps the spirits inside your bottles twist your perception. I have cooked countless meals in this kitchen, and there has been no shortage of life and laughter." Lord Michael turned towards Dorothea, a mix of anger and despair in his eyes. "Life and laughter? Ha! Do you dare speak of such things in the face of imminent doom? You are all blind to the dark tide that grows stronger within these walls." The servants exchanged exasperated glances, their patience wearing thin. Lord Michael's erratic behaviour had grown tiresome, and they longed to return to normalcy. The butler decided to intervene, albeit hesitantly. "My lord, perhaps it is time to enlist the help of a doctor. You have been troubled for far too long, and we worry for your well-being." Lord Michael patted Timothy on the shoulder, his voice a sad whisper. "A doctor cannot heal the wounds that lie within me. This darkness, this death, it consumes me. I brought it into this manor, and only I can set it right." The servants exchanged sympathetic glances, their hearts aching for their lord's suffering. They had all witnessed the toll his demons had taken on him, but they still couldn't bring themselves to believe his claims of death haunting Buckingham Manor fully. Lord Michael's drunken laments resonated through the majestic halls as the night continued. The servants listened, not out of genuine belief but out of pity for the tortured soul before them. They hoped their lord would find solace and the darkness that tormented him would finally be defeated. Little did they know that their scepticism would soon be tested, and they would discover that sometimes the most unsettling truths lie beneath the surface of even the most elaborate delusions.

CHAPTER 8 18

Lakshmi was beginning to acquaint herself with life in prison. Her situation didn't become any less bleak. With each day that passed, the feeling of hopelessness bloomed. She had no one on her side, and this feeling was confirmed each day that passed without any visitors. The only bright side of each day was the unusual friendship she'd struck with the prison porter, Mr Simmons. He would bring freshly brewed tea for them both to enjoy every evening. At first, Lakshmi had hesitated to initiate any conversation with him; she'd been wary that his friendliness was a plot to coax a guilty confession from her. That thought had been squashed immediately."I believe you're innocent. I'm old, and I could use some company." Mr. Simmons had said. Lakshmi had come to find his company valuable. Not only did they have similar views on the world, but he also brought her stories from town each evening. A smile made its way on her face as he unlocked the door to her cell, carrying a tray of freshly brewed tea and beaming at her. "Good evening, Miss Lakshmi," Mr. Simmons greeted. Lakshmi nodded. It hadn't been a good day, but she could feel her spirits lift at the thought of company and tea. The porter poured her a cup, and she took a sip, sighing at the sweet milk taste on her tongue. "Aha! Before I forget, you have a visitor today." He said, rising to his feet. Lakshmi's heart leapt in her chest. "Really? Who?" "A nice looking chap. He seemed quite concerned about you. I'll go fetch him now." A few minutes later, Mr. Simmons returned with Todd in tow. Delighted, Lakshmi shot upright from her seat at the sight of her friend." "Todd! I can't believe you're here." She said, her voice shaky with tears. She'd been so lonely for the past week, and seeing a familiar face made her feel instantly better. Todd smiled at her, and there wasn't an ounce of suspicion on his face. His unguarded mien was a relief. He wouldn't be here if he believed that she'd committed murder. "I'm sorry that it took me this long to

CHAPTER 8   20

visit you," Todd said. "It must have been a shock to you," Lakshmi murmured. Todd gave a shake of his head. "It must have been a shock to you, Lakshmi. We all know how close you were to Lady Michelle. None of the servants believe that you killed her." Her shoulders slacked in relief. She beckoned Todd over to sit. "Tell me everything that's been happening back at Manor." Todd obliged her request between sips of tea, regaling her with the situation at Buckingham. He told her of Lord Michael's drunk ramblings and how the manor had been suspended in a state of muted panic since her arrest. "I wonder what evidence they have kept me in here," Lakshmi said with a sullen sigh. "I wish I had come with valuable information," Todd said, his voice rueful. Lakshmi shook her head, reaching across the table to squeeze his hand. For a brief moment, there was a look of yearning on Todd's face. Lakshmi looked away immediately. "It's not your fault. I'm too glad to see your face anyway." At that, Todd smiled.

CHAPTER 8   21

Although, Lakshmi's next question wiped the smile off his face immediately. "How's Geoffrey doing?" She asked. If Lakshmi was being honest, it stung that he hadn't come to see her yet. They'd become close in the past few months, and just a few weeks ago, he'd confessed his feelings for her. Lakshmi was conflicted about her feelings for him, but she couldn't deny that Geoffrey meant much to her."I meant to tell you earlier," Mr. Simmons said, cutting into the conversation tentatively. "It's about Geoffrey." Mr Simmons sighed and shifted uncomfortably. "I'm afraid Geoffrey was unable to come today. He won't be able to visit you at all." The weight of his words sank into her shoulders, and they slumped. "Why not?" she demanded, her voice trembling. It was Todd who answered this time. " Geoffrey's parents have forbidden him from leaving the house. They don't want him associating with someone like you." She knew that Geoffrey's parents weren't her biggest fans at the moment, but she

CHAPTER 8   22

hadn't expected that he would let them stop him. Geoffrey was strong-willed. He did whatever he wanted without letting his family's expectations control him. Lakshmi exhaled a sharp breath. "How could he believe them? He should know that I would never do anything like that." On a different day, Todd might have chimed in to say something scathing about Geoffrey whenever the chance arose, but this time, he didn't, sensing Lakshmi's turmoil. "I'm here for you, Lakshmi." He said. Mr. Simmons shook his head. "Lakshmi, I know this is difficult to swallow, but hear me out. Geoffrey is just a young man influenced by his parent's beliefs. He may not fully understand the impact of their decision on you." She scoffed. "Geoffrey has never let that stop him." She reached for her tea and set it back down. It had gone cold. "Gave him some time. Perhaps he'll come around." Mr. Simmons said. A glimmer of determination flashed in Lakshmi's eyes, and she clenched her fists in her lap. "You're right,

CHAPTER 8   23

Mr. Simmons. I cannot let this setback define me. I will fight for my freedom and prove my innocence."Mr. Simmons smiled, pride glimmering in his eyes. "That's the spirit, Lakshmi. Remember, even in the darkest moments, there is always a faint glimmer of hope. Hold onto that, and it will guide you through." "Who needs Geoffrey anyways?" Todd attempted, keeping his voice carefully lit. "I will stick by your side, Lakshmi. I'll try to find out what evidence is against you. You'll be out of here in no time, I promise." Forcing a smile, Lakshmi nodded. She was starting to feel a little better. Mr. Simmons was right, and she needed to stay hopeful. Hope was all she had left anyway. Back at Buckingham Manor, mother and son sat in the quiet comfort of the drawing room, bathed in the soft orange glow of the setting sun. Lady Grace's elegant posture relaxed as she sipped her tea, watching Geoffrey fidget nervously in his chair. She had detected unease in his voice earlier in the day, and now

CHAPTER 8   24

her intuition whispered that something serious troubled him. "Geoffrey, my darling, you seem preoccupied," Lady Grace ventured, her voice filled with gentle concern. "Is something other than what we discussed bothering you, my dear?" Geoffrey shifted uncomfortably, a knot forming in his stomach as he stared into his cup of tea without finding solace. The gravity of his current predicament weighed heavily on his heart, burdening him with detangling a web of complications. "Mother, I need to talk to you about Lakshmi." His voice wavered slightly, betraying his inner turmoil. Lady Grace set her cup down, leaning forward attentively. "Lakshmi again? What about her, Geoffrey?" she asked, observing her son with a curious gleam in her blue eyes. Taking a deep breath, Geoffrey summoned the courage to articulate his thoughts. "Mother, I have realised that our suspicions against Lakshmi are unfounded. She is innocent, wrongly accused of a crime she did not commit." Lady Grace's eyebrows furrowed as she tried to comprehend her son's assertion. She wasn't a woman who liked to be proven wrong. "Geoffrey, you have always had a compassionate soul, but be cautious with your words," Lady Grace replied, her motherly concern. "What evidence do you have to support this assertion? Remember, the vial of poison was found in her room." Geoffrey shook his head adamantly. "Lakshmi would never do that, mother, especially to someone she cherished so much. The real culprit must have planted the vial in her room." Lady Grace gasped in outrage, and her hand flew to cover her mouth delicately. "How dare you make such accusations, Geoffrey?" "You know Lakshmi yourself. She's knowledgeable, far too much that she would leave evidence behind if she did commit the crime. Someone framed her, and they're still in this house." Geoffrey affirmed. His mother was silent for the longest time, and when she finally spoke, her voice was taut with fury. "We're going through a difficult time in

CHAPTER 8 26

this family. It's not the time to point fingers and make baseless accusations. As the only son of this family, your first concern should be our entire household, to keep us together." "If you would listen—" "No, Geoffrey, you listen to me. I won't hear any more of this nonsense again." Lady Grace snapped. Geoffrey felt frustration well up in him. He knew getting through to his mother would be difficult, but he hadn't expected her to be so stubborn. He rose to his feet angrily. "I won't let Lakshmi take the fall for a crime she didn't commit. I will do everything in my power to save her." Without another word, he stormed angrily from the room, ignoring his mother's pleas to return. Geoffrey stormed out of the imposing mansion, his face a mask of frustration and anger. The echoes of his words with his mother still rang in his ears. He could hear the familiar cadence of her voice, filled with disappointment and concern, as she pleaded with him to change his ways. But at that moment, all her words turned to meaningless, irritating noise. The cool night air embraced him as he marched aimlessly through the sprawling estate. Moonlight cast long shadows across the manicured lawns, mirroring the uncertainty that plagued his troubled mind. Thoughts unbidden rose, tearing at his soul like gnarled claws. He found himself in the dimly lit study, surrounded by shelves filled with dusty books that had long been forgotten. As his stormy gaze grazed over them, he couldn't help but remember his father, Lord Michael. Memories consumed him, taunting his wounded heart. Geoffrey's palm traced the embossed leather cover of an old journal, once treasured by his father. With a frustrated sigh, he pulled the book closer, hoping to find solace or perhaps a buried answer within its pages. His father had always been a distant figure, lost in his world of alcohol and misery, and Geoffrey feared he was doomed to follow in his footsteps. The first sip burned his throat, the fiery liquid leaving a smouldering trail in its wake. The

CHAPTER 8 28

bitterness of the alcohol seemed to echo his bitterness towards his father, and yet, paradoxically, it drew him closer, drawing him into the torment that had plagued Lord Michael's life. "Damn it, I hate myself for this," Geoffrey muttered under his breath, his voice heavy with frustration as he stared at the drink in his hand. "Why... why must I turn out just like him?" His words hung heavily in the room, carrying the weight of his deepest fears. The spectre of his father loomed over him, a constant reminder of the path he desperately yearned to avoid. As the liquid coated his senses, Geoffrey's thoughts blurred, his emotions dull as if smothered by a thick fog—a sliver of respite washed over him, a temporary release from the storm consuming his mind. Yet, deep within, he knew this was not the answer. It was merely a temporary numbing of his pain, an escape that led only to further despair. Geoffrey allowed himself to unravel with each swig, his tongue loosening and his thoughts spilling forth without reservation. Rants weaved through the air, fueled by frustration and self-loathing. "I have everything anyone could want," he muttered bitterly, his voice tinged with desperation. "But what good is it if I'm just a mere reflection of that wretched man? The mighty Lord Michael, a sorry excuse for a father... and now his failures haunt me." Silence enveloped the room, the weight of his words hanging thickly in the air. In the dim light, the man staring back at him through the glass appeared a lost soul, yearning for solace from the inferno he had inherited. As the alcohol coursed through his veins, memories of his childhood danced before his eyes. The drunken ramblings, the shattered furniture, and the constant apologies that never held any genuine remorse. They had seared their mark deep into his being, carving an unforgettable sense of doom. "I won't let it consume me," Geoffrey muttered, his voice laced with steely determination. "I won't allow his legacy to

CHAPTER 8 30

dictate my future."He slammed the empty glass onto the desk, the sound shattering the silence that enveloped the room. Slowly, he rose from his seat, his legs heavy and unsteady. Hatred and resolve mingled in his weary eyes as he glanced around the room, the remnants of his father's life surrounding him. With a final glance at the abandoned journal, Geoffrey mustered the strength to step away, to break free from the cycle that threatened to trap him. He stumbled towards the door, steadfast in his resolve to chart a different path. Geoffrey's heart was heavy with conflicting emotions as he emerged into the moonlit night. The taste of alcohol hung on his lips, but he washed it away with the cool breeze that whispered through the trees. In the darkest corners of his mind, the shadows of his father still lingered, but he wouldn't let them define him. He had the power to forge his destiny and rise above the legacy that haunted him.

CHAPTER 8   31

CHAPTER 2

The thick iron bars stood tall and imposing, casting long, forbidding shadows across the dimly lit corridor. Lakshmi's heart pounded as she took another step into her new reality – a prison cell. The heavy smell of dampness and despair filled the air, and she struggled to steady her nerves. Leaning against the cold stone walls, Lakshmi surveyed her surroundings. The cell was small, barely fitting a bed, had a small stainless steel sink, and had a shared toilet. Wooden planks for a makeshift desk and chair were nestled in a corner, offering her a meagre sense of normalcy. She marvelled at the portraits of family and friends that adorned the walls, keeping memories alive amidst the sea of grey and gloom. As she settled onto the thin mattress, the reality of her situation began to sink in. It had been a while since she got to the prison, yet her sentence remained elusive. The monotony of prison life became her constant

CHAPTER 8   32

companion, the minutes stretching into an eternity as she anxiously awaited news of her fate. Lakshmi sat alone in the prison dining hall, her mind drifting between the present and the vivid memories of her past. As a first-time offender, the chaotic and violent environment terrified her every day. She had hoped to find solace and friendship behind these daunting walls, but her dreams were shattered at every corner. On this particular day, as she quietly enjoyed her meal, she couldn't help but feel the eyes of her fellow inmates boring into her. Uncomfortable shivers ran down her spine, telling her that something sinister was about to unfold. She tried to ignore it, hastening her bite into a piece of lukewarm bread.

Just as she was about to take another bite, her solitude was interrupted by a loud clatter of trays hitting the floor. Startled, Lakshmi turned her gaze towards the disturbance and found herself face-to-face with a group of dangerous-looking women. They were known as the Black

Widows, infamous for their brutality and love for confrontation. Lakshmi had been careful to keep out of their path until now. Their leader, a woman named Ramona, stepped forward, eyes filled with malice. Her voice was laced with venom as she hissed, "Well, well, well, what do we have here? A little newbie trying to fly under the radar?" Lakshmi's heart pounded as the Black Widows slowly encircled her. Fear seeped into her veins, paralyzing her body. She tried to utter a word, but her voice refused to escape her trembling lips. Ramona swung her fist, connecting it sharply with Lakshmi's jaw without warning. Pain exploded across her face, but she refused to let the tears fall. She knew showing weakness would only fuel their savage amusement.

Another woman, Alicia, joined in, delivering a swift kick to Lakshmi's stomach. The force knocked the air out of her lungs, leaving her gasping for breath. She curled on the floor, desperately shielding herself from the onslaught

CHAPTER 8   34

of blows raining down upon her fragile body. As the minutes turned into an eternity, every kick and punch intensified, diminishing her strength gradually. Lakshmi's vision began to blur, and the world around her faded into darkness. Just as she was on the brink of losing consciousness, the sound of running footsteps echoed through the hall. A group of prison guards rushed in, overpowering the Black Widows. With swift precision, they pulled the attackers off Lakshmi and pinned them to the cold, hard floor. Lakshmi's blurry eyes locked onto the face of one of the guards, a kind-hearted woman named Maya, who had shown compassion towards prisoners before. She knelt beside Lakshmi, her calm, reassuring voice cutting through the din in the room.

"Stay with me, Lakshmi. Help is on the way," Maya said softly.

Lakshmi swallowed hard, gripping Maya's hand with whatever strength remained. "Why? Why did they do this?" Her voice was barely a whisper, her words laced with disbelief and pain.

Maya's eyes filled with empathy. "Sometimes, people act out of fear or jealousy. It's a cruel world in here, Lakshmi. But don't worry, justice will prevail."

As Lakshmi was carefully lifted onto a stretcher, she caught a glimpse of the emptiness in Ramona's eyes. At that moment, she realized that the Black Widows were just as broken and damaged as she was. Their cruelty was a last-ditch attempt to claw their way out of their demons.

Lakshmi's first encounter with the hardened inmates left her feeling vulnerable and exposed. Some pitied her, while others eyed her suspiciously, leaving her to navigate this treacherous environment alone. Each day, she fumbled through the rigid routine, learning to blend into the fabric of prison life.

Her second taste of the brutal fights that took place within the prison walls arrived

CHAPTER 8   36

unexpectedly, just days after the first, one fateful evening. A riot had erupted in the courtyard, plunging the prison into chaos. Lakshmi was caught in the crossfire, desperate to escape the violence that consumed her surroundings.

Leaving her cell, Lakshmi ventured into the fray, her heart pounding in her ears. Chaos reigned as inmates clashed with one another, their pent-up frustrations boiling into an explosive display of rage. In the distance, Lakshmi spotted a fragile figure being cornered by a group of ruthless inmates.

Driven by instinct, she rushed to the woman's aid. "Leave her alone!" Lakshmi's voice trembled, but determination fueled every word. The attackers turned their attention towards her, their faces contorted with malice. She took her stance with unwavering courage, ready to protect the defenceless woman.

A ferocious brawl ensued, blows raining down upon Lakshmi from all directions. Pain seared through her body as fists collided with her face and ribs. She fought back fiercely, her years of self-defence training guiding her every move. Despite the torrent of injuries, she never lost sight of her mission - to protect the vulnerable. Finally, the chaos subsided, leaving a trail of broken bodies and shattered spirits in its wake. Lakshmi stood battered but victorious, gasping for breath amidst the stillness that followed the storm. The woman whom she had risked her safety to save now stood beside her, tears streaming down her face.

"Thank you," the woman whispered, her voice trembling with gratitude. "I owe you my life."

Lakshmi smiled weakly, her heart swelling with a newfound sense of purpose. She knew that adapting to this life in prison would be difficult, but the knowledge that she could make a difference kept her fighting.

Days slowly turned into a week, and with each passing moment, Lakshmi's strength and resilience grew. She encountered countless

CHAPTER 8   38

battles – physical, emotional, and psychological - as she navigated the unforgiving prison walls. Bruises adorned her body like badges of honour, war wounds that told a story of a warrior refusing to back down. In the prison library, amidst the hushed whispers and worn-out books, Lakshmi discovered solace. She found an escape within the words inked on yellowed pages – a brief reprieve from the harsh reality that ate away at her spirit. Books became her sanctuary, transporting her to different worlds where she could forget the cold embrace of her cell for a moment.

Lakshmi sought comfort in her fellow inmates, forging unlikely friendships amidst the shackles of their shared fate. They shared stories and dreams, providing each other solace in the darkest hours. They became a lifeline in a place where hope seemed futile, reminding Lakshmi that she was not alone.

Lakshmi clung to the remaining fragments of hope as the days stretched into eternity. She recalled the words of her lawyer - the wheels of justice turn slowly, but they do turn. In the depth of her despair, she held onto the belief that her sentence would eventually come. Until then, she would fight the battles within the prison walls, determined to adapt, grow, and emerge stronger.

Though her future remained uncertain, Lakshmi refused to surrender to the despair that had swallowed many others. She was determined to use her time in prison to redefine her purpose, to become an instrument of change, even within the confines of her cell.

And so, as she lay on her narrow bed, her scars and bruises a testament to her resilience, Lakshmi whispered a promise to herself. She would be ready for whatever lay ahead. Let the world take its time, she thought, for she would be prepared to face it head-on when her sentence finally arrived Days later after her rescue attempt. She received a letter from Geoffrey.

CHAPTER 8   40

"Dear Lakshmi," it began, its contents etched with the unmistakable eloquence of Geoffrey, her dear friend and confidant. "I write to you eagerly with news that might light a beacon of hope amidst the darkness. Through a mutual acquaintance, a certain Mr. Simmons, I have ascertained some essential information that could help you regain your freedom."

Lakshmi clutched the letter tightly, her eyes scanning each carefully crafted word. Geoffrey had always been a man of intellect and resourcefulness, and his involvement meant a plan was in motion. "Mr. Simmons, a well-respected and connected individual, has informed us that he holds great influence within the judicial system," the letter continued. "He has agreed to lend us his assistance and oversees the necessary legal processes to uncover the truth behind your imprisonment. I understand that the wait may be unbearable, but please know we are fighting for you."Tears welled up in Lakshmi's eyes as she read Geoffrey's words.

Finally, here was someone who believed in her innocence and was willing to go to great lengths to prove it. It was a glimmer of hope amidst the haze of despair that had consumed her for so long.

Days turned slowly into weeks, and Lakshmi waited eagerly for further updates. The prison seemed to grow colder, the walls closing on her like a vice. The guards continued their relentless cruelty, looking for any opportunity to exert their power over the vulnerable prisoners. And then, another letter arrived. This time, it was from Todd, a loyal friend who had stood with her throughout their shared struggle. Todd was a man of action, never one to shy away from danger or hardship.

"Lakshmi," his letter began, "Geoffrey has informed me of the progress being made, and I've taken it upon myself to gather any additional evidence that could aid in your defence. I've worked tirelessly, digging through old records and talking to individuals who might

CHAPTER 8   42

know something about the true culprit."

Lakshmi's heart swelled with gratitude. Todd's dedication and loyalty were unwavering, his determination resonating through his words. It reminded her that she was not alone and that people worked tirelessly to bring her justice.

In the following pages, Todd detailed the information he had uncovered. Each conversation and interaction he recounted painted a clearer picture of the perpetrator. The depth of his investigation was astounding, a testament to his unwavering commitment to her cause.

A newfound strength coursed through Lakshmi's veins as she read Todd's words. She knew now that the suffering endured in this desolate prison would not be in vain. There was a purpose—a reason to cling to her battered body and take the torment inflicted upon her.

As the days passed, Lakshmi's body grew weaker, and her spirit tested with each passing day. Yet, deep within her, an ember of resilience glowed, fueled by the certainty that freedom was within her grasp.

The final letter arrived on a day when despair threatened to engulf Lakshmi. The words were simple yet powerful, carrying the promise she awaited. "Lakshmi," it read, "the wheels of justice are turning slowly. Be assured, dear friend, that we have not forgotten you. Soon, the truth will be revealed, and you shall be freed from this prison of lies and deceit. Hold on a little longer, for our resolve has never been stronger."

Lakshmi clutched the letter to her chest, relief streaming down her face. She had endured the suffering, the beatings, and the humiliation with the knowledge that a brighter tomorrow beckoned. The promise of freedom resonated through her being, altering how she perceived her present reality.

At that moment, Lakshmi knew she was no longer a prisoner but a warrior awaiting her deliverance. She would endure, for she now had

CHAPTER 8 44

a purpose—a mission to reclaim her life, expose the truth, and ensure justice prevailed.

And so, she sat in her cramped prison cell, her body battered but her spirit unyielding. The anticipation of freedom coursed through her veins, a beacon of hope that guided her through the darkest nights. Bound by the promise of those who believed in her, Lakshmi resolved to fight until she walked free once more.

Geoffrey sat in his dimly lit and cluttered study, a sense of frustration hanging heavily in the air. Ever since Lakshmi had been unjustly imprisoned, he had been tirelessly searching for clues and information that would lead him to the person responsible for framing her. His efforts had proven to be in vain, as with each passing day, the walls of her prison seemed to close in tighter around him. The sound of a knock on the door broke Geoffrey from his thoughts. With a sigh, he rose from his chair and made his way to answer it. Harrison stood on the doorstep, a tall and lanky man with deep creases etched into his forehead.

"Geoffrey, I've just returned from my investigations," Harrison said, his voice filled with weariness. "I've spoken to all the key witnesses and combed through every available evidence, but it's as if the person who framed Lakshmi was never there. There are no leads, no clues, nothing."

A wave of frustration washed over Geoffrey as he clenched his fists. "How can that be? There must be something we're missing, someone who knows more than they're letting on."

Harrison nodded solemnly. "That possibility cannot be ruled out. I'll continue digging, but I fear we may run out of options."

As Harrison departed, Geoffrey's thoughts turned inward, plagued by doubts. He had dedicated his life to seeking justice, but the more he sought the truth, the further it slipped from his grasp.

Just as Geoffrey settled back into his study, another knock echoed through the room. He

CHAPTER 8   46

opened the door to find Nicholas, a wiry man with a nervous twitch.

"Geoffrey, I've been investigating the late-night visitors to the prison, hoping to uncover any potential connections to Lakshmi's case," Nicholas said, his voice quivering with anxiety. "But all my leads have led to dead ends. Each person I interviewed seemed unconnected to the crime, and none knew anything useful." Geoffrey's frustration rose to the surface, his hands trembling. "Is it possible that someone is deliberately blocking our every move? Someone who does not want Lakshmi to be freed?"

Nicholas nodded gravely, wiping the sweat from his brow. "That seems to be the most plausible explanation. A web of secrecy surrounds Lakshmi's framing, and whoever is responsible is skilled at hiding their tracks."

Left alone once more, Geoffrey's bewilderment grew. It felt like each passing day brought disappointment and a tightening noose around his throat. His mind raced, trying to make sense of the puzzle that eluded him at every turn.

The sun had long set when the third knock reverberated across the wooden door. This time, it was Jonathan, a stout man with a reputation for uncovering secrets.

"Geoffrey, I've been tracking the financial transactions surrounding Lakshmi's case," Jonathan explained, booming and confident. "But I've hit a roadblock. Everything appears clean, no irregularities, no payments made to witnesses, nothing suggesting foul play."

Geoffrey's frustration boiled over, his voice tinged with desperation. "How can this be? How can someone orchestrate such an elaborate setup and leave no trace?"

Jonathan's eyes gleamed with determination as he held up a slender piece of paper. "There is one thing I found, however. It's a name, a seemingly insignificant one. Claire Thompson. She seems to be on the periphery of Lakshmi's case, offering small pieces of information here

CHAPTER 8   48

and there. Perhaps she holds the key, no matter how faint."

Hope flickered in Geoffrey's heart as he seized the paper, examining the name scribbled upon it. Maybe, just maybe, this would be the breakthrough they had all been waiting for.

Days kept passing, which was something Geoffrey hated, taken that Lakshmi was still in there as the days passed. Geoffrey and his loyal companions tirelessly pursued every lead related to Claire Thompson. But each lead dissolved into another dead end, dispersing their hopes like smoke in the wind.

Lakshmi remained locked behind iron bars, her spirit dampened but not defeated. Communication with her was scarce, as if the world conspired to keep them apart, to weaken their resolve. Geoffrey's frustration grew, matched only by his unwavering determination.

As he sat alone in his study, surrounded by stacks of papers and dusty books, Geoffrey's gaze lingered on a small picture of Lakshmi.

Her laughter seemed distant, a memory fading into the abyss of uncertainty. But he refused to let it slip away entirely.

There was still a glimmer of hope, no matter how faint. Geoffrey knew he couldn't give up, no matter how many dead ends they encountered. He would continue to search, to question, to fight. The truth was buried beneath the layers of deception, waiting to be unearthed.

By the time Geoffrey and Todd had exhausted their options and ran out of clues about the real culprit, Lakshmi had been on hold for about two weeks. With each passing day, the weight of uncertainty on their shoulders grew heavier, and they realized they were running out of time to find the truth.

Geoffrey knew they needed a breakthrough, a lead that could help them uncover the real culprit behind the heinous crime. He couldn't bear the thought of Lakshmi being locked up while the actual criminal roamed free. He was determined to find justice.

CHAPTER 8 50

Ultimately, Lakshmi's desire for company trumped her desire to keep her head down. It had been weeks already, and it had become more challenging to hold on to hope. Geoffrey's letter had reassured her, but with each day that passed, nothing happened. She'd written letters to her family back in India, but there no way of knowing when they would receive them or if they would. She imagined that her father was worried about her.

She imagined the crease of his brows with each day that passed, and no word of hers reached his ears. Her mother would try to reassure him, but it would be a facade to hide her anxiety. Lakshmi's heart clenched every time she thought of Meena, her sister. Perhaps it was a good thing that her letters hadn't reached them. She couldn't imagine how devastated and betrayed her father would be once he found out that his daughter had been thrown in jail by his benefactors. She could do much for herself while she was behind bars. Perhaps it was high time that she stopped keeping to herself.

She glanced around the room and noticed a group of individuals clustered together on the other side. Their dishevelled appearance and hardened expressions suggested they had been in this place for quite some time. Curiosity piqued within her as she approached them cautiously.

"Hello," Lakshmi spoke softly, trying not to startle them. "I'm Lakshmi. May I join you?"

The group turned their attention towards her, assessing her with sceptical eyes. One woman, who seemed to be the pack's leader, stepped forward. She had a rugged appearance, with unkempt hair and a hardened gaze.

"And what makes you think we would want your company?" She grunted, crossing her arms.

Lakshmi took a deep breath, gathering her courage. "We may not have much reason to trust each other, but we're all prisoners here. And sometimes, even the most unlikely alliances can result in survival."

CHAPTER 8 52

The woman, whose name was Celeste, seemed to be slightly intrigued by Lakshmi's words. She glanced at her companions, a silent question poised on her face. The others exchanged glances as well before finally nodding in agreement.

"Fine," Celeste grumbled. "But don't think for a second that we're your friends."

Lakshmi nodded, grateful for the small victory. As she settled among them, she listened intently as they shared their stories, the conversations flowing with intense and lengthy discussions. They were diverse, each with tales of misfortune and wrong choices.

There was Sabrina, an ex-convict who had fallen in with the wrong crowd in her earlier days. Her actions had brought her back to these very walls. She had learned that sometimes, what seemed like a shortcut to success was just an illusion.

Then, there was Kavita, a toughened woman with an air of resilience. She had once been a victim of human trafficking, forced into a life of exploitation. Over time, she had found the strength to break free from her captors, but her past still haunted her.

Next was Brenda, a woman who had grown up in poverty and became susceptible to the allure of easy money through crime. She had made choices that had consequences, and now she languished in this cold, damp place, contemplating where her life had veered off course. As they shared their stories, Lakshmi couldn't help but empathise with these individuals. Despite their bad decisions, she saw the glimmers of kindness and desperation behind their rugged exteriors. She realized they were human beings deserving another chance beneath the rough exterior.

Days passed, and during their time together, Lakshmi found solace in the companionship of her unlikely allies. They would spend hours talking, sharing their dreams, and consoling each other in moments of despair.

CHAPTER 8   54

Lord Michael stood outside the entrance of Lakshmi's ancestral home, feeling entirely like an outsider. The air was heavy with anticipation as he prepared for the delicate task ahead. It had been months since he had left India, taking Lakshmi with him to join him in England. Now, he stood there, feeling a tumult of emotions within him. He glanced at the invitation letter in his hands, reminding himself of the delicacy of the situation. Upon receiving the news of his visit, Lakshmi's parents invited Lord Michael to their home, eager to hear updates about their beloved daughter. Yet he knew he couldn't reveal the painful truth that had unfolded in Buckingham Manor.

As he entered the humble house, he was greeted by the rich aroma of incense. The plainness of the surroundings only reminded him of the stark difference between this world and that of his English estate.

Lakshmi's father, Rajan, a stocky man with a warm smile, approached Lord Michael, his eyes filled with hope and concern. "Welcome back, my lord. We have been eagerly awaiting your arrival. How fares my daughter in the grand Buckingham manor?" he asked, twisting his fingers in nervous anticipation.

Lord Michael understood the gravity of Rajan's words and felt a pang of guilt, but he knew he couldn't disclose the truth. "Fear not, Rajan Ji," he replied reassuringly, adopting an impeccable British accent. "Lakshmi is thriving in England. She has adapted well to the customs and traditions of our noble society. She is cherished by all who meet her."

Rajan's face lit up momentarily, but a shade of concern lingered. "But why has she not written to us, my lord? Surely, she would wish to keep us informed of her happiness and well-being?"

Lord Michael shifted uncomfortably, realizing he was navigating a treacherous path of lies. "You see, dear Rajan, the obligations of our high society can be overwhelming. Lakshmi has found herself engrossed in the constant demands

CHAPTER 8   56

of social engagements. She barely has time to think, let alone write."

Rajan nodded hesitantly, still not entirely convinced by Lord Michael's explanation. "I trust you will convey my love and blessings to her. Her mother and I pay our humble respects to the esteemed members of the Buckingham manor. We eagerly await the day we may visit her ourselves."

Lord Michael felt a twist in his gut, knowing he couldn't let that day come. "Of course, Rajan Ji. She often speaks of her deep longing to be reunited with her family. But the hectic schedule of the manor and the pressures of society have made it incredibly difficult for me to arrange her return to India. Just be assured that she is treated with the utmost care and respect."

Lakshmi's mother, Lata, a graceful woman with deep-set eyes, joined the conversation. "My Lord, we worry for our daughter's well-being. Her absence has left a void in our hearts. We know not what she is truly enduring. Could you please provide us with some peace of mind?" Her voice was filled with desperation, her eyes imploring Lord Michael to be truthful.

Lord Michael could feel the weight of the lies he had woven threatening to unravel. He took a deep breath and precisely replied, "Lata, I give you my word as a gentleman that Lakshmi is cherished in Buckingham Manor. She resides in the finest quarters and is surrounded by the finest of our society. There is nothing you should worry about."

Lata's eyes brimmed with unshed tears, and she reached for her husband's hand for support. "If only we could see her for ourselves, Lord Michael. To hold her in our arms and ensure her happiness. Is there any chance you could arrange a brief visit for us?"

Lord Michael's heart ached at her words, but he composed himself and said convincingly, "I promise you, my dear Lata, that I will make every effort to facilitate a visit. However, you must understand the complexities of our society

CHAPTER 8   58

and the expectations placed upon Lakshmi. Rest assured that she is surrounded by all the love and care one could desire."

As Lord Michael continued to exchange pleasantries with Lakshmi's family, his mind was filled with inner turmoil. He could feel the weight of his deception growing heavier with each passing moment. He knew the truth would need to be revealed eventually, but for now, he had decided to bear the burden alone.

☐

CHAPTER 3

Todd stood outside the county jail's towering walls, taking a deep breath to steady his nerves. He glanced down at the crumpled piece of paper in his hand, on which he had painstakingly pencilled down every detail of the news he was about to deliver to Lakshmi. After all these weeks, seeing her again filled him with a strange mixture of excitement and trepidation.

The heavy iron gates creaked open, and he stepped inside the bleak and sterile visiting area. The air felt heavy with despair, amplified by muffled sobs and the occasional echo of harsh words from the nearby cells. His footsteps seemed to echo like a drumbeat as he went to the designated booth where he would meet Lakshmi. Todd's heart pounded in his chest, threatening to burst out at any moment.

As he approached the booth, he caught sight of Lakshmi, looking haggard and worn. Her once-lustrous hair hung limp and dull around her face, emphasizing the deep circles under her eyes. He took a moment to gather his composure before sitting opposite her, being separated only by the thick, soundproof glass.

"Lakshmi," he breathed, his voice barely above a whisper. She raised her head, her eyes widening in surprise.

"Todd? Is it you?" Her voice was filled with hope and confusion as if she couldn't believe her eyes.

"I told you that I'd be back." Todd reminded her.

Lakshmi leaned closer in her seat. "What's going on outside? Have the police found anything? Please, Todd, tell me. I can't bear this torment much longer. I'm tired of enduring this place any further."

He nodded, his heart aching at the torment she had endured. "Your court date has finally been fixed. It's scheduled for a month from now. The legal proceedings have been moving slowly, but you have a chance to prove your innocence. Just hold on."

A mix of emotions flickered across Lakshmi's face - a spark of hope mixed with fear and doubt. "Well, do you think they'll believe me? After everything that's happened?"

Todd took her hands through the glass, offering his silent support. "Lakshmi, it's been tough, but you must hold onto hope. The evidence is on your side, and I believe in your innocence. We will fight tooth and nail to prove it."

Tears welled in Lakshmi's eyes, glistening like diamonds in the harsh overhead lighting. "Thank you, Todd. Knowing that someone believes in me gives me the strength to keep going."

They sat silently for a moment, their gazes locked, communicating a thousand unspoken words. Todd's mind raced, grappling with what was at stake. He had to find a way to break her out of this prison of despair.

"Lakshmi, I've been talking with a few

CHAPTER 8   62

lawyers who specialize in wrongful convictions," he started, trying to keep his voice steady. "They believe they can help us build a strong defence, but we need your cooperation. We must gather as much evidence as possible to prove your innocence." A flicker of determination crossed Lakshmi's face. "I will do whatever it takes, Todd. I will fight tooth and nail to prove that I did not commit the crime I'm accused of."

Todd smiled, feeling a glimmer of hope ignite within his chest. "That's the spirit! We cannot falter in our pursuit of justice. We must dig deep, investigate every angle, and present a compelling case in court."

Lakshmi's eyes shone with a newfound determination. "Tell me, Todd, where do we start? What can I do from inside these walls?"

Todd leaned closer, his voice dropping to a mere whisper. "We start by looking for inconsistencies or loopholes in the prosecution's case against you. We dive deep into your alibi, scrutinize every piece of evidence, and track down potential witnesses who could provide an alternate version of events."

Lakshmi nodded, her mind already racing through the mazes of possibilities. "I remember a few suspicious things that happened that day. Maybe they're connected somehow. Maybe there's something we missed."

Todd's face brightened with a glimmer of excitement. "Yes, exactly! We must piece together the puzzle and expose the hidden truth. Remember, Lakshmi, the truth will always come to light, no matter how long it takes."

They spent hours in the visiting area, engrossed in conversation. Todd unveiled his plans, discussing strategies and potential leads, while Lakshmi provided every detail she could recall. The glass that separated them felt like a mere inconvenience; their minds merged into a singular force of unstoppable determination.

As the visitation hours drew close, Todd reluctantly rose from his seat, a renewed fire

CHAPTER 8 64

burning within him. "Lakshmi, we will do everything we can to secure your freedom. Have faith, my dear friend. We will triumph over this darkness together."

Lakshmi wiped the stray tear that had escaped her eye, nodding with a newfound sense of purpose. "Thank you, Todd, for being my light in this abyss. I will never forget your unwavering belief in me." Todd smiled, holding her gaze for a moment longer before turning to leave. "Stay strong, Lakshmi. I will be back soon. We have a month to prepare, a month to fight for justice. This is the beginning of a path leading you back to where you truly belong." With a final glance over his shoulder, Todd stepped through the heavy iron gates, leaving behind a ray of hope that would cast its glow upon the darkest corners of the jail. The battle for Lakshmi's freedom had begun, and nothing would deter him from achieving justice for his beloved friend. The courtroom buzzed with anticipation as Lakshmi sat anxiously in the wooden pew, her hands trembling with nerves. The weight of the past few days had taken its toll on her, but hope was rekindled as the judge finally entered the chamber. "Miss Lakshmi," the judge's voice boomed across the room, calling her to rise. "After careful consideration of the plea made by your defence, the court decides to grant you bail." A wave of relief swept over her, and tears rose. She had been imprisoned for weeks, trapped unjustly in a storm of suspicion. Finally, she had a glimpse of freedom."However, your bail comes with certain conditions, given the severity of the charges. You will be allowed to reside in the Buckingham residence until your trial. There, under the protection and surveillance of the authorities, you can remain distanced from the Buckingham family while awaiting trial. This will ensure the safety of all parties involved." Lakshmi let out a tiny sigh of relief. She wasn't exactly keen to be back at the scene of a crime, but that way, it would be easier to solve the

CHAPTER 8 66

mystery of Lady Michelle's murder. Across the courtroom, she caught Todd's eye, his lips quirked up in a brief smile. The judge cleared his throat. "But let it be known that any violation of these conditions will result in immediate bail revocation." With the judge's decision, the courtroom erupted into whispers and hushed discussions.

Feeling hopeful and apprehensive, Lakshmi exited the courtroom and was escorted to the Buckingham residence by a diligent officer. As she arrived at the grand estate, its towering gates swung open. A mixture of emotions flooded her heart: gratitude for the court's leniency and sorrow at the separation from her dear family. Inside the residence, Constable Reynolds, a tall man with broad shoulders, gave her a stiff nod. "Welcome, Ms. Lakshmi. I understand this may be a challenging transition for you, but rest assured, we have taken utmost care to ensure your safety."

Lakshmi nodded, appreciating the detective's

empathetic tone. "Thank you, constable. I'm grateful for your efforts in bringing me here safely."

The world's weight seemed to lift off her shoulders as she took her first breath of fresh air. Yet, a lingering sadness held her captive as she realized that she hadn't seen nor heard from Geoffrey, her close friend, throughout her entire ordeal.

As she made her way further into the house, Lakshmi spotted Geoffrey standing in the hallway, as still as the paintings of his ancestors that hung on the walls, seemingly lost in thought. He looked different, wearier, as if a burden weighed heavily on his mind.

"Geoffrey? Is that you?" Lakshmi called out uncertainly.

Startled, Geoffrey's head whipped around, his eyes widening in surprise. "Lakshmi!" he exclaimed, jumping up from his spot. "You're free! Thank goodness!"

Her heart was filled with both relief and

CHAPTER 8   68

confusion. "Yes, I am," she replied hesitantly. "But where were you all this time, Geoffrey? I needed you, and you were nowhere to be found."

Geoffrey's expression softened, guilt painted across his features. "I'm sorry, Lakshmi," he said, his voice tinged with regret. "I should have been there for you. I know I failed as a friend."

Her eyes filled with unshed tears, Lakshmi nodded in acknowledgement. "Why, Geoffrey? What happened?" He hesitated for a moment, his gaze fixed on the ground. "I... I didn't visit you in jail because I couldn't bear seeing you like that, trapped behind those walls," he confessed, his voice barely above a whisper. "But that doesn't excuse my absence. I should have mustered the courage to be there for you." Geoffrey couldn't bring himself to tell Lakshmi the truth, making his parents look bad.

Lakshmi's heart swelled with a mixture of sadness and understanding. "It's all right, Geoffrey. I know it must have been difficult for you," she said gently. "But what brings you here now? And why do you seem so troubled?" Geoffrey met her gaze, his eyes filled with a flicker of determination. "I came to apologize, Lakshmi, but I also have news," he said, his voice taking on a serious tone. "I posted your bail. I heard that the court granted you bail. I couldn't do anything less than pay it." Surprise washed over her, the enormity of his words sinking in slowly. "You did what?" Lakshmi exclaimed, her voice carrying a mix of shock and gratitude. "Geoffrey, you didn't have to do that for me."

Gently placing a hand on her arm, Geoffrey offered a reassuring smile. "I did it because you mean the world to me, Lakshmi. Our friendship has always been something special, and I couldn't bear to see you suffer for a crime you didn't commit," he admitted, his voice full of sincerity. Tears welled up in Lakshmi's eyes, trailing down her cheeks. She reached out, embracing Geoffrey tightly. "Thank you, my

CHAPTER 8 70

dear friend. You have no idea how grateful I am," she whispered, her words laced with emotion. Pulling away from the embrace, Geoffrey's expression grew serious once again.

"There is more, Lakshmi. I think I have an idea who set you up." Her eyes widened with renewed intrigue. "Tell me, Geoffrey. Who would do such a thing?" He shook his head. "I can't tell you yet. It is still a hunch." Lakshmi hesitated. "I know that you're on my side, Geoffrey." Despite him refusing to share his suspicion, she still trusted him. "I will tell you more once I have substantial proof." He said. "All right then." She paused, considering the weight of her following words. "I have something to ask you, though." Eager to earn her forgiveness, Geoffrey bobbed his head willingly. "Whatever you want." "I need you and Todd to work with me to uncover the truth. To find the evidence that will prove my innocence. It's time to set things right." Geoffrey blinked. "Surely you can't be serious.

Work with that stable boy?" Lakshmi flinched. "I didn't know you were this classist. I'm not noble either, in case you forgot." Geoffrey sighed. "I apologize, and you know what I mean. I don't like him."

"But—"

He shook his head, cutting off her words. "I would do anything for you, Lakshmi, almost anything. But I'm sorry, I refuse to work with a man who covets your affection like I do."

Without another word, Geoffrey brushed past Lakshmi. She sighed, watching him go. After Lakshmi's conversation with Geoffrey, Reynolds led her through the grand hallway of the Buckingham residence, adorned with elegant paintings and antique furniture. The atmosphere felt both luxurious and isolating. As they reached a cosy parlour, Lakshmi's eyes caught a glimpse of a slender woman in her late forties sitting by the fireplace. "Lakshmi, dear," the woman's voice was soothing, "I'm Lady Bridgette Wayland. I've been informed of your

CHAPTER 8   72

situation and will oversee your stay here. Please, have a seat." Lakshmi sat down, her eyes flickering with curiosity. "Thank you, Lady Bridgette. I appreciate your kindness," she replied, trembling with restrained emotions. Reynolds stood nearby, observing their conversation, ready to intervene if necessary. "Lakshmi, I assure you, although you are separated from your family and friends, you are under our protection. I know it may seem daunting, but this arrangement serves the interests of justice and the safety of all parties involved," Lady Bridgette comfortingly explained. "I understand, but being away from my family and friends pains me. They need me, and I am desperate to be with them during this trying time," Lakshmi's voice trembled with unshed tears.

Constable Reynolds stepped forward, interjecting. "Ms. Lakshmi, you and the Buckingham family's safety is our highest priority. We have taken all the necessary measures to ensure their well-being. Trust us when we say this is temporary until the situation clears and the truth becomes apparent."

Geoffrey paced back and forth in his study, his mind buzzing with frustration. The suggestion Lakshmi had made earlier before today was still lingering in his thoughts, irritating him like an incessant itch. He couldn't fathom why she would propose working with Todd, especially after everything that had happened between them, knowing that they were some competition to each other. The very idea made his blood boil. Briefly, he wondered if Lakshmi bore romantic feelings for Todd. She had a soft spot for the stable hand, and he couldn't deny their friendship.

Geoffrey's anger grew stronger as the sun dipped below the horizon, casting long shadows across the room. It wasn't just the suggestion that incensed him but its implications. It felt like a betrayal, a mockery of the trust he and Lakshmi had built over the months. Unable to

CHAPTER 8   74

contain his emotions any longer, Geoffrey stormed into his home prison room where Lakshmi was reading, determination etched on his face. He could see the surprise in her eyes as she looked up from her book, sensing the storm brewing within him.

"Lakshmi, I need to talk to you about what you said earlier," Geoffrey began, his voice laced with anger. "How could you possibly think I would work with Todd after everything he's done to me?" Lakshmi placed her book down gently and looked up at Geoffrey, her expression a mix of concern and apprehension. "Geoffrey, please sit down. There are things we need to discuss calmly without jumping to conclusions." Geoffrey huffed, resisting the urge to dismiss her plea. He begrudgingly sat across from her, his frustration evident in the harsh lines on his face. "I don't need an explanation, Lakshmi," Geoffrey continued, his voice sharp. "Todd has tried to sabotage our relationship countless times. Hell, he even sees me as a competition. How can you expect me to trust him?" Lakshmi leaned forward, her voice calm but firm. "Geoffrey, I understand your reservations; believe me, I do. But this is an opportunity to set aside our differences and work towards a common goal." Geoffrey shook his head, his frustration boiling over. "A common goal? I don't think so." Lakshmi's face took on a pained expression, and her voice softened. "Geoffrey, please try to see beyond your anger. This collaboration would open doors for both of us, allowing us to work this case more easily."

Feeling a glimmer of doubt, Geoffrey hesitated. He couldn't deny the truth in this, and there was nothing he wanted more than to help prove Lakshmi's innocence.

The room fell silent as Geoffrey pondered Lakshmi's words. Deep down, he knew she wasn't trying to betray him or his feelings. He understood her intentions, yet allying with Todd seemed impossible.

CHAPTER 8   76

After what felt like an eternity, Geoffrey sighed heavily, his anger deflating like a balloon. "Fine."

Lakshmi's eyes widened with delight, her smile illuminating her face. "Geoffrey, I'm so glad you're considering this. It means the world to me."A smile bloomed on his face before promptly fading. "I'm doing this for your sake only. I'm not going to become friends with Todd." Lakshmi nodded. "I'm not expecting that. I wouldn't have asked the both of you to work together if you weren't my only allies." Geoffrey's smile softened. "You'll always have me by your side." The look on his face hinted at feelings deeper than spiritual ones. Lakshmi looked away. "I know. I'll always be lucky to have you as a friend, Geoffrey." Friendship was all she could offer for now. Now wasn't the time for romance in her life. The morning sun cast a muted glow through the lace curtains of the elegant dining room at Buckingham Manor. The table was adorned with fine china and silverware, but the atmosphere within was strained. Geoffrey sat rigidly in his chair, barely touching the sumptuous breakfast. Lord Michael and Lady Grace exchanged concerned glances. Geoffrey's eyes darted nervously between his parents, his usually composed demeanour fraying at the edges. The tension in the room was palpable, suffocating the usual air of luxury.

Lord Michael cleared his throat, breaking the uneasy silence. "Geoffrey, my son, you seem quite preoccupied this morning. Is something amiss?" Geoffrey pushed a piece of toast around his plate, avoiding eye contact. "Nothing of consequence, Father. Just a restless night, that's all."Lady Grace observed him closely, her piercing gaze cutting through the pretence. "Restless nights and distracted mornings have become quite the pattern lately, Geoffrey. Care to enlighten us on the cause?" A heavy sigh escaped Geoffrey's lips as he reluctantly met his mother's eyes. "It's this accusation against

CHAPTER 8   78

Lakshmi, Mother. I can't shake the feeling that she's innocent, and I cannot stand idly by while an injustice unfolds."

Lord Michael's stern expression darkened. "Geoffrey, I've warned you about meddling in this matter. Lakshmi stands accused of murdering my mother. This is not a place for sentimentality." Geoffrey's jaw tensed, his resolve unyielding. "Father, I cannot abandon Lakshmi in her hour of need. I've seen the evidence, and it doesn't add up. I believe there's more to this than meets the eye." Lord Michael's eyes narrowed, a mixture of frustration and disappointment etched on his face. "You jeopardize the honour of this family with your misplaced sympathy. Lakshmi was my mother's nurse, Geoffrey. Don't forget her place." Geoffrey was adamant. "Father, I can't turn a blind eye to injustice either." "Enough, I want to hear nothing on the matter again." Lord Michael slammed a fist on the table. Geoffrey barely held his flinch in time. Without finishing his meal, Geoffrey abruptly stood, the scraping of his chair against the parquet floor echoing through the room. As Geoffrey made to leave, Lady Grace's voice, sharp and accusing, cut through the air. "Geoffrey, is there more to this than a mere sense of justice? Have you developed feelings for that girl?" The question hung in the air, a heavy cloud casting shadows over the room. Geoffrey's face flushed, his eyes betraying a mix of defiance and vulnerability. "Mother, this is not about personal feelings. It's about seeking the truth and ensuring justice prevails," he retorted, his voice strained. Lady Grace rose from her seat, her elegant stature imposing. "Don't play the innocent with me, Geoffrey. Your infatuation with Lakshmi has clouded your judgment. You jeopardize everything we've worked for." Geoffrey squared his shoulders, a determined glint in his eyes. "I won't abandon someone in need, Mother. I'll find the truth and prove Lakshmi's innocence." His mother scoffed, and the sound

CHAPTER 8 80

echoed sharply. "Don't be ridiculous."

"I'm inspecting the farms today," Geoffrey announced abruptly. Technically, he would be making rounds, but not for the reasons his parents thought. He'd agreed to join forces and work with Todd at Lakshmi's insistence, and he wasn't looking forward to it, but he couldn't deny that an extra hand wouldn't help in his amateur investigation. He and Todd would be speaking to a few of the servants today. Geoffrey was particularly suspicious about his father's impromptu decision to search the manor house—and, subsequently, Lakshmi's room, which led to the discovery of the arsenic bottle in her room. He didn't think his father was behind Lady Michelle's mother. Not even a little bit. Lord Michael was many things: cowardly, impulsive and alcoholic, but he loved his mother. But perhaps the natural killer had given him the idea to search the manor. If Geoffrey could find out who that person was, he'd find the killer. "But you've barely touched your food." Lady Grace said. "I have things to do,"

Geoffrey repeated slowly. He was still cross at his parents. Specifically, his mother. He couldn't understand how easily she'd turned against Lakshmi. Initially, she'd taken Lakshmi under her wing and treated her like a friend rather than a servant. And now, she was cold and indifferent. Now, she looked tired. His mother always wore elegant airs at breakfast or an important gathering. She tried to hold on to that dignified aura, but the slight frown on her face gave her away. Deciding to shift the conversation away from Lakshmi, Geoffrey turned to his parents as they followed him to the entrance hall. "I've been neglecting the estate lately. I think it's time I inspect the farms and ensure everything is in order." Lady Grace seized the opportunity to steer the conversation in her desired direction. "Geoffrey, while you're tending to the affairs of Buckingham Manor, it might be wise to distance yourself from

CHAPTER 8 82

unnecessary distractions." Geoffrey arched an eyebrow, sensing the veiled meaning in his mother's words. "Distractions, Mother?" Lady Grace's gaze hardened. "It's time you set aside any affections that might hinder your responsibilities. Focus on your duties as heir, and ensure your decisions are guided by reason, not sentimentality." The implication hung in the air, and Geoffrey felt the weight of his mother's expectations. "Mother, my commitment to Buckingham Manor is unwavering. I assure you, I will prioritize the estate above all else." However, he wouldn't ignore his loyalties to Lakshmi. Lady Grace's smile returned, though with a touch of coldness. "That's what I like to hear, Geoffrey. A responsible heir understands the importance of making sacrifices for the greater good." Lord Michael nodded approvingly. "A commendable decision, Geoffrey. It's crucial to uphold the standards of Buckingham Manor. Go and see that our lands are flourishing." Lady Grace smiled faintly.

CHAPTER 8   83

"It's heartening to see Geoffrey taking a more active role in managing the estate. Perhaps he's finally realizing the responsibilities of being the heir." Lord Michael agreed, "Yes, it's about time he embraced his duties. The future of Buckingham Manor rests on his shoulders." Lady Grace couldn't resist a pointed remark, her tone laced with a subtle warning. "Speaking of the future, Michael, perhaps we should consider Geoffrey's marriage. A union with a suitable match would secure the legacy of Buckingham Manor." Lord Michael glanced at Lady Grace, considering her words. "You may be right. A strategic alliance could strengthen our standing. We'll have to start exploring suitable matches for Geoffrey." "Are you two going to pretend like I'm not here?" Geoffrey asked incredulously. In the opulent dining room of Buckingham Manor, the tension escalated with each passing moment. Geoffrey was frustrated with his parents' insistence on his imminent marriage. His anger boiled beneath the surface,

CHAPTER 8   84

threatening to erupt. "There's no need to rush into marriage, Mother. Father is still young and healthy, and there's time for me to consider my options," Geoffrey declared, the undertones of rebellion lacing his voice. Lady Grace, however, remained unyielding. "Anything can happen, Geoffrey. Your grandmother's murder was a stark reminder of the unpredictability of life. It's essential to secure the future of Buckingham Manor sooner rather than later." Geoffrey flinched at the vulgarity of his mother's words. Even Lord Michael looked taken aback by the audacity. "That is not the same case; you know it, mother." He insisted. Lady Grace ignored his words and took a sip of her tea, which had no doubt gone cold judging from the grimace that crossed her face briefly. "Either way, my point still stands." Geoffrey's eyes flashed with defiance. "I won't be pressured into a union for convenience. I'll choose a partner when the time is right." In attempting to mediate, Lord Michael urged, "Let's not dwell on this matter now. Geoffrey, you have your duties to attend to. Focus on the estate, and we'll discuss your future soon." But the seed of discontent had been sown. With a resentful sigh, Geoffrey stepped away from his seat. "I have other matters to attend to." Lady Grace, exasperated, couldn't let him leave without a parting remark. His mother was equally headstrong. "Geoffrey, the stability of Buckingham Manor depends on your decisions. Don't let your stubbornness jeopardize everything we've built." Ignoring her words, Geoffrey stormed out of the dining room, leaving the door to swing shut behind him. The estate gardens offered little solace as he navigated the manicured hedges, frustration and resentment bubbling within him. Entering the stables, the familiar scent of hay and horses provided a temporary refuge. Spotting Todd tending to a chestnut mare, Geoffrey approached with a determined stride. "Todd, we have work to do. I do need your help to prove Lakshmi's innocence after all." His voice was

CHAPTER 8   86

bitter. The day had barely started, and it was already a terrible one. First, he'd rowed with his parents, and now he would be forced by his promise to Lakshmi to work with Todd.

"What has got your breeches in a twist this early?" Todd asked sarcastically.

"I suppose that it's beneath you to be mature." Geoffrey snapped.

The stablehand's eyes narrowed. "I promised to do anything to help Lakshmi so I won't say anything about that. But you need to get over your superiority complex, and your status means nothing to me while we work together to help Lakshmi." The dining room felt colder in the aftermath of Geoffrey's departure. Lady Grace turned to her husband, "Michael, our son is stubborn and reckless. His defiance will tarnish the reputation of Buckingham Manor." Lord Michael, torn between familial loyalty and the burden of legacy, sighed heavily. "Grace, we must tread carefully. Geoffrey is headstrong, but we cannot afford a scandal. Let him cool off, and we'll address this issue later." "That seems to be your go-to every time there's conflict, pushing it away until it explodes in our faces." His wife said, feigning a light tone. Wearied by the persistent tension, Lord Michael cast a disapproving look at Lady Grace. "Your comment about Lady Michelle was thoughtless, Grace. We don't need reminders of tragedy during these trying times." Lady Grace, unyielding, responded with a piercing gaze. "Michael, you're too lenient with Geoffrey. His stubbornness could bring disgrace upon Buckingham Manor. We can't afford such recklessness. For goodness sake, he fancies himself infatuated with that girl."

Contrary to what his wife thought, Lord Michael was equally displeased with Geoffrey. He'd always shown a softness towards Lakshmi from the very beginning. Perhaps those feelings should have been squashed back then, but he'd looked the other way. Now, he couldn't agree with his wife when she would rub it in his face.

CHAPTER 8 88

Lord Michael sighed, grappling with the complexities of parenthood and legacy. "He's our son, Grace. We must balance guiding and allowing him to make his own choices." But Lady Grace wasn't ready to relent. "His choices could tarnish the reputation of this estate. We've worked too hard for him to throw it away for the sake of misplaced ideals." "He's just having a bit of fun with that girl. Surely, you can't be afraid he'll decide on a whim to marry her. Even if she wasn't a murderer, she is still beneath him in status. Geoffrey's misguided affections aren't anything to worry about." Lord Michael said with a dismissive wave. Lady Grace's laughter was cold. "You never take these things seriously until they get worse." "I'm trying to focus on the things that matter." Lord Michael argued. She scoffed. "Let's not forget your role in this, Michael. Your constant indulgence in alcohol has done nothing but contribute to the sorry state of Buckingham Manor." His wife's words struck a nerve. He clenched his fist around his spoon.

Lord Michael, taken aback, felt a surge of anger. "Grace, you've crossed a line. My struggles are not to be weaponized in our family disputes." But Lady Grace persisted, her tone biting. "Perhaps if you focused on managing the estate instead of drowning your sorrows, we wouldn't be in this predicament." The accusation hung in the air, a stark reminder of the internal battles plaguing Buckingham Manor. Shocked by the sudden events, Lord Michael took a moment to collect his thoughts.

"My struggles are my burden to bear, Grace. Don't use them to deflect from the real issue– our son's future and the accusations against Lakshmi." Lord Michael said. The air in the dining room hung heavy with unresolved tension as Lord Michael and Lady Grace locked eyes in a battle of wills. The accusation about Lord Michael's struggles with alcoholism lingered, a painful truth hanging in the space between them. Before the verbal sparring could

CHAPTER 8 90

escalate further, the grand doors of the dining room creaked open, revealing a servant poised to clear the remnants of the tumultuous breakfast. The intrusion abruptly paused the heated exchange, the servant hesitating at the doorway, sensing the charged atmosphere. "Shall I clear the table, my lord, my lady?" the servant inquired, cautiously navigating the delicate situation. Lord Michael nodded curtly, still processing the weight of Lady Grace's words. "Yes, proceed."

The servant entered quietly, glancing at the noble couple's strained expressions. The clinking of silverware against fine china filled the void, a stark contrast to the silence that had settled between Lord Michael and Lady Grace. Lord Michael broke the uneasy silence as the servant efficiently cleared the breakfast remnants. "We will continue this discussion later, Grace. For now, let us attend to the matters at hand." Lady Grace, though still visibly perturbed, consented with a terse nod.

The servant swiftly exited, leaving the couple alone once more, the echoes of their disagreement lingering in the room. he heavy oak door groaned in protest as Lord Michael pushed it open, revealing the dimly lit expanse of his study. The room exuded an air of antiquity, with mahogany bookshelves lining the walls, their shelves burdened by volumes that seemed to hold the wisdom and follies of generations past. A worn Persian rug, a tapestry of muted colours, lay beneath the imposing mahogany desk, bearing witness to the weight of countless decisions. As Lord Michael stepped over the threshold, the door closed behind him with a soft thud, sealing off the outside world and trapping him in the confines of the room. The flickering flames of the hearth cast a warm, dancing glow that played upon the surfaces of leather-bound tomes and the gleaming surface of the polished desk. He approached the desk, the intricate carvings under his fingertips a familiar touchstone. The ledger lay open, its

CHAPTER 8   92

pages filled with the meticulous records of Buckingham Manor's fiscal struggles. Each entry marked their declining fortunes and whispered the challenges that shadowed the once-prosperous estate. Lord Michael lowered himself into the plush leather chair, its well-worn surface moulding to the contours of his weary frame. The study, bathed in the amber light, became a cocoon of solitude where the echoes of family disputes reverberated only as distant whispers. His eyes, a reflection of the burdens he carried, scanned the ledger with a heavy heart. The numbers blurred, and for a moment, he was transported to another conversation – a memory etched in the recesses of his mind. "Michael, you tend to drown your sorrows. It's a weakness that won't serve you well," his mother's voice echoed, a haunting reminder of her wisdom. With a sigh that seemed to echo through the ages, Lord Michael muttered to himself, "Mother wouldn't be proud of what I've become, especially with how I've handled the estate since her murder." The room, a silent witness to the struggles within, seemed to hold its breath as Lord Michael grappled with the ghosts of the past. The soft crackling of the hearth provided a backdrop to his musings, a comforting lull that heightened the moment's gravity. His thoughts drifted to a vow made aloud, an oath to bring justice to the accused Lakshmi. "I'll make Lakshmi pay for her crimes. It's the least I can do to honour Mother's memory," he declared, the determination in his voice masking the shadows of doubt that danced in the recesses of his conscience. The desk, a bastion of authority and responsibility, hid a secret within its confines. Lord Michael's hand reached for the drawer, its pull a familiar ritual. The hidden bottle, a covert ally in his struggle against the weight of his existence, emerged. The crystal glass, a vessel for solace and torment, clinked softly as the amber liquid flowed. Lord Michael raised the glass to his lips, the first sip burning with the

CHAPTER 8 94

bitterness of regrets and unresolved pain. The warmth that followed, however, offered a deceptive sanctuary, a fleeting respite from the burdens that seemed impossible. As he stared into the depths of the glass, a war waged within him – between the obligations of the present and the escape promised by the amber elixir. With its hallowed silence, the study bore witness to a man trapped in the clutches of his demons, seeking refuge in the amber embrace of a bottle that held the promise of oblivion. The air crackled with unspoken animosity, the silent clash of wills echoing in the cavernous space. Though a haven of familiarity for Geoffrey, the stables became an arena of simmering tension as he faced Todd. His day was about to get worse, he thought darkly. He didn't like the stable hand and was too friendly to Lakshmi.Geoffrey didn't like that this common person was his competition for Lakshmi's attention. Frankly, he didn't see why Lakshmi would harbour feelings for him. Todd was mild in manner and looks.

"Todd, I've no patience for your insolence. Regardless of our grievances, we must work together to clear Lakshmi's name." Todd's rugged countenance marked by defiance shot Geoffrey a disdainful glance. "Don't mistake our collaboration for camaraderie, milord. I've my reasons to distrust the likes of you."Geoffrey's jaw clenched, his displeasure palpable. "Your suspicions won't change the truth, Todd. Lakshmi is innocent, and we need to find out why Lord Michael suddenly ordered that search of the manor."The stablehand's eyes narrowed, a stubborn resolve etched in his expression. "You nobles think you're entitled to everything. Why should I trust you?" A heavy silence hung between them, each word an unspoken accusation. Despite their common goal, their discord was a chasm neither seemed willing to bridge. After a moment of tense silence, Geoffrey exhaled sharply. "We don't have to like each other but need answers. Let's call a truce for Lakshmi's sake." Todd's gaze

CHAPTER 8 96

wavered, the rigid lines of his face softening slightly. "Fine, truce it is. But don't think this erases our differences, milord." Geoffrey suggested, "We should speak to James, the chief butler. He's been with the family for years and might know why my father ordered the search."

Todd grunted in agreement, his scepticism lingering. "Fine, but don't think I'm doing this for you, milord. Lakshmi's the only reason I'm involved." The two unlikely allies approached the manor, a silent pact binding them to a common cause. The grandeur of Buckingham Manor loomed over them, a reminder of the social chasm they sought to navigate in pursuit of justice. Entering the servant's quarters, they located James, the chief butler, while organizing silverware. His greying hair and meticulous demeanour betrayed years of dedicated service to the Buckingham family. Geoffrey took the lead. "James, good morning."

James looked up and gave a slight bow. "Milord. How can I be of service?" Geoffrey tried to adapt a casual tone. "As you must know, I was out of the house on the day of the search. I wondered if you knew why Lord Michael ordered the search leading to Lakshmi's predicament. Any insight you can provide will be invaluable." James regarded them with a discerning gaze, his years of service instilling an air of authority. "Milord, it's not my place to question Lord Michael's decisions. But if you seek information, perhaps the servants can shed light on the events leading to that search."

Still harbouring his reservations, Todd added, "We need specifics, James. Someone must know why the manor was turned upside down that day." James sighed, a subtle acknowledgement of the complexities at play. "Very well, I'm unsure what spurred Milord to call for a search. I was busy with my duties. But Marie was the first to know." Marie was the head cook of the manor; she was known for her exceptional cooking, but she was as quiet as a mouse outside the kitchen. Geoffrey never

CHAPTER 8   98

interacted much with the other servants but could count the number of times he'd spoken to Marie. He wasn't sure that she would talk to them willingly. He exchanged a look with Todd. They were both thinking the same thing. However, they would try. Geoffrey would go to any lengths to prove Lakshmi's innocence. A few minutes later, they found themselves in the kitchen.

The kitchen was a bustling hive of activity, hummed with the synchronized rhythm of the culinary staff at work. The aroma of sizzling food filled the air, and Geoffrey regretted walking out of breakfast. Marie, the head cook, presided over this culinary symphony. Her grizzled hands moved with practised precision, the clatter of utensils and the sizzle of ingredients composing a culinary overture. The orchestration stilled as Geoffrey and Todd entered, and eyes turned to the unexpected visitors. Geoffrey, though accustomed to the hierarchical norms of the household, felt the weight of Todd's scrutiny, a reminder of the discord that lingered beneath the surface. Navigating the uneasy truce, he approached Marie, her weathered face betraying a lifetime of service.

"Milord." Marie's voice was a rasp that told Geoffrey just how little she spoke. Her eyes darted warily from Geoffrey's to Todd's. For a second, he hesitated. "May we speak outside?" His words only caused the cook to tense even more. But she couldn't refuse. He was, after all, the next in line to be Lord of the manor. She bobbed her head in a nod and allowed herself to be led outside the kitchen. "Marie, we need your help. We seek the truth about the search that implicated Lakshmi," Geoffrey implored, his voice carrying the weight of earnestness. Marie's eyes flickered with trepidation, her apron-clad form shrinking under the collective gaze of her peers. "Milord, I appreciate your concern but can't risk my position by speaking out." Geoffrey, attempting reassurance, stated,

CHAPTER 8   100

"Marie, I assure you, we're here to uncover the truth. Your honesty won't go unnoticed." The cook's gaze darted between Geoffrey and Todd, distrust etched in the lines of her face. Geoffrey's noble stature seemed to heighten her anxiety. Sensing her fear, Todd cut in with an empathetic expression that softened the edges of his rugged features. "Marie, we're not here to harm anyone. Your words could help an innocent girl. Trust us, please." Something in Todd's earnest appeal seemed to resonate with Marie. She hesitated, torn between loyalty and fear. Geoffrey, however, couldn't help but feel scorned. He'd tried to speak kindly to her, but it hadn't worked. Yet, she seemed to want to open up to Todd. The realization that Todd was likeable didn't sit well with him. After a lingering pause, Marie relented, her voice a hushed undertone amid the kitchen clatter. "All right, milord. I'll help in whatever way that I can." Secluded in a corner, Marie divulged the clandestine details of that fateful day. "Lord

CHAPTER 8   101

Michael was frantic when he ordered the search. He'd just returned from receiving daily letters from town." His mind racing, Geoffrey sought to decipher the significance of his father's urgency. "Letters from town? What could be in those letters that would prompt such a drastic action?" Todd, contemplative, suggested, "Maybe the manor's postman knows something. If Lord Michael was agitated after receiving his letters, it's worth investigating." Geoffrey nodded in agreement, grappling with a mix of frustration and intrigue. "Let's speak to the postman, then. Marie, thank you for your help." The head cook's eyes widened in surprise at his gratitude. Geoffrey felt uneasy. Not only was Todd quickly liked, but he was starting to think that he was the opposite. Geoffrey's thoughts swirled with emotions as they left the kitchen. Todd's ability to garner trust unsettled him. He didn't have time to dwell on the idea, however. The manor's postman, a wiry figure with grizzled features, was discovered in the

CHAPTER 8   102

servants' quarters. Geoffrey, determined to uncover the truth, approached with a blend of authority and curiosity. "Good day. We seek information about the letters Lord Michael received on the day of the search. Can you shed light on this matter?" Geoffrey inquired his tone a mix of diplomacy and insistence. The postman, wary of the unexpected inquiry, eyed Geoffrey with a hint of suspicion. "I deliver the mail, milord, nothing more. What happens afterwards is none of my concern." Todd's tone, measured and congenial, interjected, "We're merely trying to understand the events that led to Lakshmi being framed. Any information you can provide will be invaluable." Geoffrey felt a flicker of irritation at his interference. Todd's approach also swayed the postman, who sighed in reluctant surrender. "Speak quickly then. I've got rounds to finish," the postman grumbled, a tone of reluctance in his voice. "The letters," Geoffrey said, his voice curt with impatience. The postman's gaze shifted between Geoffrey and Todd, gauging the sincerity in their eyes. After a lingering silence, he sighed, resignation softening his expression. "I can't say which letter unsettled Lord Michael, but he must still have it. That's all I know." Geoffrey, a flicker of frustration in his eyes, pressed further. "Can you at least give us an idea of the nature of the letters he receives daily? Any recurring themes or peculiarities?"

The postman shrugged, his demeanour hardened by years of silent observation. "Mostly business correspondence, occasional personal letters. Lord Michael keeps his affairs close to his chest. If you want more, you'll have to ask him yourself. He's your father, after all."

As the postman's reluctance hung in the air, Todd picked up on a subtle cue – a suggestion wrapped in discretion. "Maybe it's time for a private conversation with Lord Michael, milord. He might hold the answers we're looking for." Geoffrey, conflicted by the implications of such a confrontation, hesitated. The unspoken truths

CHAPTER 8   104

lingering in the conversation weighed heavily on him, a reminder that the path to justice was uncertain. The postman, observing their indecision, ventured a veiled suggestion. "Some doors are meant to be opened alone, milord. Sometimes, you'll find what you seek by facing the source directly."

As they left the postman's quarters, the narrow passage echoed with the shroud of secrets and the creaking uncertainty of their mission. "You're going to talk to your father, right?" Todd asked. "Why would he tell me the truth? He's the one pushing for Lakshmi to be found guilty." Geoffrey snapped. Most people would have flinched at Geoffrey's anger but not Todd's. "Well, we have no choice. Not when he might hold the truth in his hands." "I can't just ask my father about the letter without revealing my true intentions. It could jeopardize everything." Geoffrey argued. Todd, pragmatic and persistent, responded, "If you can't ask him directly, maybe you need to find that letter yourself. Break into his study." The suggestion, though practical, sent a shiver down Geoffrey's spine.

The idea of infiltrating his father's private sanctuary. Delving into the secrets concealed within, he tapped into a well of fears he dared not confront. He turned to Todd, eyes blazing with anger. "How dare you suggest that? Do you have no respect for your lord?" Todd raised his chin. "My loyalties are with Lakshmi. Yours should be, too. If you're torn about seeking justice, perhaps you shouldn't deceive Lakshmi with false intentions to help." Geoffrey clenched his fists, reining in the urge to hit Todd's smug face. "I'm doing all I can to help Lakshmi. I'm going against my parent's orders. Don't you dare talk to me about loyalty?"

Todd, undeterred, countered, "Milord, sometimes the truth is the only way to set things right. If there's any chance of proving Lakshmi's innocence, we need that letter." I know that." Geoffrey ground out. "Then you

CHAPTER 8   106

know what to do," Todd said. Bristling at the obvious challenge in the other man's voice, Geoffrey said, "And if I don't?" "I'll do anything for Lakshmi. I think you know what that entails." Todd said. Geoffrey didn't dignify Todd with an answer. Later that evening, Geoffrey met with Todd and Lakshmi in the garden as they'd agreed. The manicured garden was bathed in the soft hues of dusk, the delicate fragrance of blooming flowers mingled with the gentle rustle of leaves as the trio reconvened beneath the sprawling branches of an ancient oak. The air was tranquil, even with the distant chirping of birds. But it did nothing to soothe the conflict that Geoffrey was warring with.

Geoffrey's expression was a tapestry of emotions, recounting the day's revelations to Lakshmi. Lakshmi, her eyes reflecting both curiosity and caution, listened intently. "So, Geoffrey, tell me everything. What did the postman say? What's our next move?" Geoffrey, his gaze a mosaic of conflicting emotions, took a deep breath before launching into the intricate narrative. "The postman wasn't sure which letter unsettled my father, but he's certain Lord Michael still has it. Todd suggested approaching my father directly, but that carries risks. Then, there's the daring idea of breaking into his study." Lakshmi, her fingers absently tracing the petals of a nearby rose, absorbed the revelations with a measured intensity. "Approaching your father is risky, but it could yield answers. Breaking into his study is equally risky. What do you feel is the best course of action?" Torn between familial duty and the allegiance forged with Lakshmi, Geoffrey grappled with the decision.

"I'm inclined to try talking to my father first. Maybe he'll be more open than we anticipate. If that fails, then we can consider more drastic measures." Lakshmi, her gaze penetrating, studied Geoffrey's expression. "Are you sure about this, Geoffrey? It could strain your relationship with your family. I don't want to be

CHAPTER 8 108

the cause of discord." Geoffrey, touched by her concern, offered a small smile. "Lakshmi, you've become a part of this, a part of my world. I can't stand by and do nothing. If talking to my father is a way to help you, then it's a risk worth taking." With a sense of determination in his eyes, Geoffrey answered, "I'll start by talking to my father." He tried to infuse some confidence in his voice, but he failed. "What if he refuses to share anything?" Lakshmi asked hesitantly. Geoffrey sighed in contemplation. "I'm not sure how he'll react. Todd suggested breaking into his study to find the letter, but I can't shake the fear of what I might discover." He shot a glare at Todd, who shrugged. "Lakshmi is the one who might go to prison if we don't prove her innocent, but all right, worry about your father instead," Todd said mildly. "Todd, please." Lakshmi cut in before Geoffrey could retort. He felt ridiculously pleased that she'd interfered on his behalf. Lakshmi, her slender fingers tracing the petals of a nearby rose, responded with a quiet resolve. "Geoffrey, you've already done so much for me. I don't want you to jeopardize your relationship with your family. If it's too much, I'll find another way." The sincerity in Lakshmi's words touched Geoffrey, a fleeting moment of vulnerability shared beneath the dappled sunlight. "No, Lakshmi, I've made a promise to you, and I intend to keep it. I'll find that letter, one way or another. If talking yields results, then we'll reconsider our options. Breaking into his study is a last resort, so don't worry."

Sensing the conversation's delicate nature, Todd excused himself with a nod, leaving Geoffrey and Lakshmi alone in the garden's tranquillity. As the silence settled between them, broken only by the gentle whisper of the breeze, Lakshmi shifted the conversation to lighter matters. "Tell me, Geoffrey, what's your favourite flower? I've always believed one can learn much about a person from their choice of bloom." Geoffrey, appreciating the diversion,

CHAPTER 8   110

mustered a smile. "Roses, I suppose. They may seem cliché, but they have an elegance, a timeless beauty that captivates me." Lakshmi, a glimmer of mischief in her eyes, plucked a velvety red rose and extended it toward Geoffrey. "A rose for the elegant lord. Quite fitting, don't you think?" Accepting the offered flower with a chuckle, Geoffrey replied, "Perhaps. And what about you, Lakshmi? Do you have a favourite flower?"

Lakshmi's gaze softened as she spoke, her fingers trailing over the delicate petals of a nearby jasmine. "Jasmine. Its fragrance is subtle yet enchanting. It reminds me of home, of the gardens in India where I used to play." The revelation sparked a tender curiosity in Geoffrey's eyes. "Tell me about your home, Lakshmi. I want to know more about the places that shaped you. Under the enchanting canopy of the ancient oak, Lakshmi's eyes sparkled with the memories of a distant world. Jealously captivated by her tales, Geoffrey leaned in with an encouraging smile. "Tell me, Lakshmi," he urged, "what was it like growing up in India? Paint me a picture of your home." A soft smile played on Lakshmi's lips as she delved into the vibrant tapestry of her past. "India is a land of contrasts, milord. The colours are so vivid in the markets that they seem to dance. Sarees in every hue imaginable, spices piled high in mounds of gold and red, and the constant hum of merchants calling out their wares." Geoffrey smiled at her words. Lakshmi had a way of captivating him with ordinary stories. He found himself wanting to know more about her life. "It sounds like a feast for the senses. What about your family? Tell me about them." Lakshmi's gaze softened with fond remembrance. "I have a sister, her name is Meena. She's relatively younger than me, but we're as close as best friends." Geoffrey leaned in, "Do you two look alike?" With a snort, Lakshmi answered, "She takes after our father. Her hair is longer than mine, and we couldn't be more different in personality. She

CHAPTER 8   112

has lofty dreams and high hopes to achieve them all." Hearing the wistfulness in her voice, Geoffrey said, "You must miss her." Lakshmi looked away, her smile fading. "Well, I miss many things about home." "Like what else?" "I miss the festivals, too, milord. Diwali, the festival of lights, was my favourite. The entire town would sparkle with lamps and candles. It was as if the stars had descended to earth." Geoffrey, enchanted by the imagery, envisioned the radiant glow of Diwali. "Festivals must have been joyous occasions. What traditions did your family follow?"

Lakshmi's fingers absentmindedly played with a nearby jasmine as she spoke. "Diwali was a time for family gatherings, feasts, and exchanging gifts. We would light oil lamps, decorate the house with vibrant rangoli patterns, and share sweets with neighbours. It was a celebration of light and love."

Geoffrey, leaning in with genuine interest, asked, "Did you have any favourite sweets?"

CHAPTER 8 113

Lakshmi's eyes twinkled as she recounted the culinary delights. "Oh, yes! Gulab jamun, jalebi, and barfi were among the favourites. The sweetness lingered for days, and we'd enjoy them with laughter and stories."

As the night deepened, the garden embraced their conversation like an attentive audience. Wrapped in the cocoon of Lakshmi's narratives, Geoffrey felt a connection to a world so distant yet vividly painted through her words.

Lakshmi, sensing his genuine interest, shared more intimate details. "There was a banyan tree near our house, milord. Its expansive roots spread like a sanctuary. I used to sit beneath it, lost in books or watching the world go by."

When picturing the serene scene, Geoffrey remarked, "A banyan tree as a sanctuary sounds idyllic. What books did you enjoy?"

Lakshmi's eyes lit up with passion. "I loved stories of adventures, distant lands, and brave heroes. They fueled my imagination and took me to places beyond the pages. It was my

CHAPTER 8 114

escape, my way of exploring worlds beyond the every day."

Genuinely engaged in the conversation, Geoffrey confessed, "I, too, find solace in stories, though mine are often tales of knights and chivalry. It's fascinating to hear about your perspective."

Lakshmi, her voice a gentle melody, replied, "Our worlds may be different, milord, but stories have a way of weaving a common thread between them. They remind us of our shared humanity."

"I like that we have things in common," Geoffrey said softly. His breath caught as he stared at her. She'd never looked more beautiful to him, with dark hair carried gently by the wind and a slight smile.

Yet, beneath the charm of their conversation, an unspoken tension lingered. Lakshmi, perceptive as ever, sensed the conflict in Geoffrey's loyalties. "You don't have to go against your parents for me, Geoffrey. I'll be fine, and I appreciate everything you've done."

Grappling with conflicting responsibilities, Geoffrey met her gaze with gratitude and turmoil. "I want to help you, Lakshmi, no matter the cost. You've become a part of my world, and I can't turn away now."

The evening sun dipped below the horizon, casting long shadows across the garden. In that fleeting moment, Geoffrey wished they were two different people leading different lives. Then he might have acted impulsively and kissed her like he wanted to right at this moment.

The following day, as the sun painted the manor grounds in hues of amber, Lakshmi sat alone at the quaint cottage where she found refuge. A simple breakfast spread adorned the table – a reminder of the quiet start to another day amid uncertainty.

As she sipped her tea, Todd appeared at the doorstep. "Mind if I join you for breakfast, Lakshmi?" he asked casually.

CHAPTER 8   116

Lakshmi gestured for him to take a seat, warmth in her eyes. "Please, Todd. It's always good to have company." She meant it, too. She was grateful that the judge had granted her bail, and the cottage was lovely, but it still felt a little like a prison. There was nobody to spend most of the day with, and she tried not to roam the estate grounds often to avoid running into Lord Michael or Lady Grace.

Todd sat at the table, and Lakshmi poured him a cup of tea. Sunlight filtered through the lace curtains, casting gentle patterns on the wooden table. The aroma of freshly brewed tea and the simple fare added a touch of comfort to the morning.

Settling into the chair with effortless grace, Todd initiated the conversation. "How did you sleep, Lakshmi? These cottages may not be as grand as the manor, but they have a certain charm, don't they?" His eyes twinkled in a teasing light. "Although I'm not exactly sleeping in any of the grand bedrooms at the manor."

Lakshmi smiled, appreciating the genuine attempt to lighten the mood. "The bed is quite comfortable, Todd. It feels like a haven amidst all that's happening."

The conversation meandered like a gentle stream as they delved into casual topics.

Todd shared anecdotes of the manor's stables, tales of horses with distinct personalities.

"The stallion, Thunder, he's a majestic creature, but as stubborn as they come," Todd chuckled, his eyes alight with fondness. "He won't let anyone near his favourite patch of grass without a playful nudge. It's like he knows he's in charge."

Lakshmi smiled at Todd's obvious affection for his job. He discussed the horses like most people talked about their lovers. "It sounds like the manor's stables are filled with human and equine characters."

Todd grinned, appreciating her engagement. "Oh, you have no idea, Lakshmi. The

CHAPTER 8   118

stablehands have their own stories, too. There's always a bit of drama or mischief, just like any other place."

At that, she laughed. "I imagine the horses squabble with each other like siblings do."

Todd leaned forward in his seat, nodding enthusiastically. "Exactly like siblings. Speaking of which, do you have siblings?"

Lakshmi's smile dimmed a little. She was homesick, and discussing her family didn't make her feel better like she thought it would. Yesterday's conversation with Geoffrey only reinforced that truth. But Todd was smiling expectantly at her, and she couldn't find it in herself to let him down. "A sister. But we rarely ever bickered; our favourite thing to do together was go to the markets to do our shopping."

Todd smiled. "I can't imagine the markets back home are like the ones here."

"In the markets, it's like being surrounded by a kaleidoscope of hues," Lakshmi mused, her eyes sparkling with nostalgia. "Every corner tells a different story, and the air is filled with the fragrance of spices and the calls of merchants."

Todd, transported to the vivid scene through Lakshmi's words, smiled. "I can almost picture it. Must be a far cry from the manor's polished halls and orderly gardens."

Lakshmi nodded, a smile gracing her lips. "Indeed, Todd. But there's a beauty in the chaos, a rhythm that becomes a part of you. It's what I miss the most. Apart from my family, of course."

She sighed, setting her tea cup down. "My family was my sanctuary, Todd. Evenings on the veranda, with the scent of jasmine, are etched in my heart."

Todd, recognizing the tender sentiment, replied with a nod. "Family is a precious thing, no matter where you are. It's what keeps us grounded, gives us strength."

Lakshmi blinked back tears. She suddenly didn't want to discuss her family anymore.

Sensing her mood, Todd reached for her hand

CHAPTER 8   120

and patted it. "I swear, I'll do whatever it takes to prove your innocence, Lakshmi."

She believed him. "I know you will. I hope we can solve this, Todd. I... I can't go back there again."

There, meaning prison. Todd seemed to know it, too. "You won't."

Lakshmi, momentarily distant, confessed, "Being locked up in prison was a struggle, Todd. The uncertainty and isolation were like being trapped in a nightmare with no end in sight."

Todd's expression softened, empathy etched into his features. "I can't imagine what that must have been like, Lakshmi. No one deserves to endure such hardship, especially not someone as kind-hearted as you."

Lakshmi, grateful for the sincerity in Todd's words, met his gaze with a nod. "Thank you, Todd. Your sympathy means a lot."

As the conversation deepened, Lakshmi could tell that Todd was itching to ask something else.

CHAPTER 8   121

Eventually, he made up his mind and did, "Has Geoffrey made up his mind about getting that letter for you, Lakshmi? I know he's wrestling with it, but it's crucial for your case."

Lakshmi, her gaze momentarily dropping to her tea, hesitated. "He's going to talk to his father first. I don't want him to jeopardize his relationship with his family, Todd. There's more at stake than just my case."

Todd, furrowing brows, couldn't hide the hurt that flickered in his eyes. "But Lakshmi, he made a promise to help you. If he backs down now, he's giving up on you. I thought he was different, you know?"

Lakshmi, her heart heavy with conflicting emotions, explained gently, "Todd, I don't want Geoffrey to ruin his relationship with his parents because of me. It's not just about giving up – it's about understanding the consequences of his actions. He has a duty to his family, just as I have to find the truth."

Todd, though still disheartened, nodded in

CHAPTER 8   122

reluctant acceptance. "I get it, Lakshmi. It's just tough seeing someone with a chance to make things right hesitate like this. I don't understand why you give him so much grace." Hurt coloured his voice.

Wincing, Lakshmi scrambled to find the right words to soothe his concerns. "Geoffrey isn't a bad person, Todd."

"While you were locked away, he didn't lift a finger to help at first." Todd insisted.

Lakshmi exhaled sharply. She understood Todd's concerns about her but knew they were also born out of selfish jealousy.

His easygoing demeanour had shifted, and tension hung in the air as he looked at Lakshmi with a furrowed brow. "Lakshmi," he began, his voice tinged with frustration and concern, "I don't get why you trust Geoffrey so easily. You barely know him, and now you rely on him to help clear your name?"

Lakshmi responded cautiously, taken aback by the sudden change in Todd's tone. "Todd,

Geoffrey was the one who posted my bail. He's also trying to help us get to the bottom of this. I believe he wants to help."

"But can you be sure?" Todd countered, his gaze unwavering. "He's a noble, part of the same system accusing you. Do you think he can guarantee justice? I doubt it."

Lakshmi sighed, a pang of conflict resonating within her. "Todd, I appreciate your concern, but Geoffrey has promised to help. We have to give him a chance."

"Promises, Lakshmi," Todd scoffed, frustration etched on his face. "Promises are just words until they're backed by action. I don't trust Geoffrey, and I don't want to see you get hurt because you're putting too much faith in him."

Lakshmi, her patience tested, spoke earnestly. "Todd, you have to understand. Geoffrey has offered his help willingly. I can't turn away someone genuinely wanting to make things right."

CHAPTER 8   124

Todd, a spark of frustration in his eyes, took a deep breath before opening up about his feelings. "Geoffrey might be helping now, but can you trust him in the long run? Will he stand by you when things get tough, or will he abandon you when it's convenient for him?"

Torn between loyalty and uncertainty, Lakshmi replied, "I don't know, Todd. I can only hope that Geoffrey stays true to his word. But that doesn't mean I should push away someone offering help based on doubts."

Todd's frustration escalated. "You're being naive, Lakshmi. Trusting someone from the same class accusing you is a risk you shouldn't take. I can help you. I promise I won't let you down."

Lakshmi, her heart heavy with conflicting loyalties, looked at Todd compassionately. "Todd, I value our friendship, but I can't dismiss the possibility of help from others. Geoffrey and I are working together, and I won't turn away support just because of

CHAPTER 8   125

suspicions."

Todd, hurt and disappointed, shook his head. "You're making a mistake, Lakshmi. Geoffrey might offer help now, but he's part of a system that oppresses people like us. Don't let his charm blind you to the truth."

Lakshmi, her resolve tested, responded firmly. "I won't abandon someone willing to stand by me. Trust has to start somewhere, Todd. I hope you can understand that."

Her words seemed to be the final push that caused Todd to snap.

He shot up from his seat, his chair scraping back on the wooden floor loudly. "Lakshmi, I can't keep pretending. I care about you, more than just a friend. I've cared for a long time."

She'd known about Todd's feelings for her for a while and valued him. How could she not when he'd been the first to believe in her innocence? But she didn't know if she felt the same feelings that he did.

"Todd, I appreciate your honesty. Our

CHAPTER 8   126

friendship means a lot to me, but I can't reciprocate those feelings right now."

Todd, encouraged by his confession, reached out to cup her face. "Lakshmi, we can be more than friends. I can be there for you in ways Geoffrey might not understand. Let me show you."

As he leaned in for a kiss, Lakshmi, caught off guard gently pushed him away. "Todd!" She shouted.

He pulled away from her with a guilty look. "I—"

She cut him off. "Please. I can't make decisions about us right now. I'm in a crisis and can't be committed to someone when I'm not even certain about my freedom!"

She wondered if her words were too harsh but decided they were not. It was better that she knew the truth than led him on.

Todd, hurt by the rejection, stepped back. "Lakshmi, I'm trying to help you. If you knew how I felt, you might see Geoffrey for what he is – a noble with his agenda."

Lakshmi, her heart heavy with conflicting emotions, sighed. "Todd, this isn't about choosing between you and Geoffrey. Right now, my focus has to be on proving my innocence. I can't afford to let personal feelings complicate an already complex situation."

Frustration etched on his face, Todd ran a hand through his hair. "You're putting too much trust in him. Can't you see that? I want to be the one by your side, not some noble who might abandon you when it suits him."

Lakshmi, her voice steady but compassionate, responded, "Todd, I value our friendship, but I can't make promises about something more. I need time to figure things out, and I hope you can respect that."

Todd, feeling the weight of unrequited feelings, nodded reluctantly. "I'll give you the time you need, Lakshmi. But don't let him break your heart. Nobles are skilled at leaving a trail of broken promises behind them."

CHAPTER 8   128

Lakshmi stood up, torn between loyalty to her friend and the uncertainty of her future. "Todd, please understand. My focus right now is on clearing my name. I hope you can support me as a friend, even if it's not in the way you want."

Todd, his frustration evident, turned to leave. "I'll be here if you change your mind, Lakshmi. Just be careful who you put your trust in."

Lakshmi sank back into the chair as the door closed behind him, her thoughts a tumultuous storm. Once a refuge, the cottage now felt like a battleground of conflicting emotions. She couldn't deny Todd's feelings, but navigating romance's complexities wasn't a priority amid her struggle for freedom.

Geoffrey was surprised to find his mother seated at the table alone for breakfast the following day. His eyes roamed the dining hall, half expecting his father to pop out from underneath the table. Lord Michael was big on family values, and usually, it took an emergency for him to miss breakfast.

Noticing his silent question, Lady Grace said, "Your father had to rush off early this morning. I reckon he'll be away the entire day."

Geoffrey nodded as he took the seat across from her. "Good morning, Mother," he greeted, trying to inject warmth into his voice.

Lady Grace responded with a nod, her gaze piercing. "Geoffrey, I must say, you've been scarce these past few days. What has been occupying your time?"

Geoffrey hesitated before crafting a reply, his thoughts lingering on his clandestine efforts to help Lakshmi. "Ah, matters concerning the estate, Mother. There have been pressing issues to attend to."

Lady Grace arched an eyebrow, scepticism evident in her expression. "Matters concerning the estate? Your duties as the heir are crucial, Geoffrey, and you can't afford to neglect them. I expect you to be more diligent in your responsibilities."

Geoffrey, feeling the weight of his double life,

nodded. "You're right, Mother. I apologize for any lapse in my duties. I'll make amends."

Lady Grace, not one to easily dismiss her concerns, leaned forward. "This is not the first time, Geoffrey. I hope there isn't something else occupying your thoughts." Her question was less than subtle. She was trying to find out if Geoffrey was still going against her.

Geoffrey attempted a calm demeanour, acutely aware of the need to divert attention. "Just the usual burdens of overseeing the estate, Mother. Nothing more."

The tension lingered as Lady Grace scrutinized him. However, before she could press further, Geoffrey quickly redirected the conversation.

"Mother, concerning Lakshmi..." He attempted. Lady Grace cut him off immediately.

Her expression hardened. "Geoffrey, I will not entertain baseless accusations against the staff. The investigation is being handled appropriately. You need not concern yourself with the affairs of the servants."

Geoffrey, frustrated by the constant resistance, persisted. "Mother, I don't understand how you can easily turn against her. You used to like her. How can you stand by and let her suffer for a crime she didn't commit?"

Lady Grace's gaze turned icy. "Geoffrey, this is not your concern. I will not allow you to jeopardize the reputation of this family for the sake of a servant. It's time you focus on more suitable matters."

Undeterred, Geoffrey pressed on. "Mother, justice is a suitable matter. I won't look the other way when I believe someone is wrongly accused. I implore you to consider the possibility of Lakshmi's innocence."

Lady Grace, her patience wearing thin, leaned back in her chair. "Geoffrey, enough of this nonsense. I've already begun looking for eligible brides for you. It's time to fulfil your duties as the heir and start thinking about your future."

A knot tightening in his stomach, Geoffrey

CHAPTER 8 132

couldn't hide his frustration. "Again, with this? I understand the importance of my responsibilities, but I can't simply ignore what I believe is an injustice. Lakshmi deserves a fair chance, and I won't abandon her."

Lady Grace, her eyes narrowing, issued a stern warning. "Geoffrey, I will not tolerate your defiance. You will cease these fruitless pursuits and focus on the path set before you. Your duty to this family comes first, and I will not entertain any more discussion."

Her expression was shuttered, and he knew better than to push. With a sigh of frustration, he tucked halfheartedly into his breakfast. He'd tried to reason with his mother and had failed. He didn't think figuring it out with his father would be better. The time for drastic resorts he has had come. He was going to break into his father's office.

Geoffrey waited until the late evening when the manor started to unwind from the day's activities. Lord Michael was still out, and

Geoffrey was confident he wouldn't return until tomorrow. Still, it didn't stop him from feeling awful. He wished he could detach himself from his loyalty to his family but couldn't.

The night draped Buckingham Manor in shadows, and as the moon cast a silver glow in the hallways, Geoffrey found himself standing outside the imposing door of his father's study. His heart pounded with a mixture of anticipation and trepidation. The need for answers had driven him to this clandestine act – breaking into his father's sanctum to uncover the secrets.

With steady hands, Geoffrey produced the keys to the study. It hadn't been challenging to swipe them out of his father's bedroom. The subtle click of the lock gave way to the muted creak of the study door, revealing the dimly lit room beyond. The faint scent of aged books and polished mahogany enveloped him as he entered.

Geoffrey's eyes scanned the room, alighting on the ornate desk where Lord Michael conducted

CHAPTER 8   134

his affairs. Moonlight filtered through the curtains, revealing a room adorned with relics of family history—a portrait of his great-grandfather hung on the wall above the desk. Those eyes seemed to follow Geoffrey as he settled in his father's seat.

Ignoring the pang of guilt in his chest, he set to work, carefully looking through the pile of letters on the desk. He glanced through a few of them briefly before discarding them. Then he thought better. Indeed, his father wouldn't leave something so important lying on his desk with other correspondence.

Geoffrey reached for one of the drawers on the desk. It only took him a few minutes of searching to find what he was looking for. The seal, broken by a careful hand, hinted at the urgency that had accompanied its delivery. Geoffrey's pulse quickened as he unfolded the parchment and began to read the anonymous message within.

"To Lord Michael Buckingham,

Lady Michelle's demise was not the result of natural causes. She was poisoned, and the perpetrator resides within the manor walls. Beware, for the danger lingers close, concealed among the servants who attend to your family's needs.

An Observer."

Geoffrey's breath caught in his throat as the weight of the revelation settled over him. The implications echoed in the silence of the study. This letter caused his father to call for a sudden search of the servants' quarters. His mind raced, connecting the dots between this letter and Lakshmi's unjust accusation. The realization struck him like a lightning bolt – the murderer, according to this anonymous Observer, was still within the manor's walls. But Geoffrey was inclined to believe that the Observer was the murderer; they were diverting all the attention away from themselves to Lakshmi.

A mixture of determination and unease fueled Geoffrey as he carefully folded the letter.

CHAPTER 8   136

Clutching the incriminating evidence, he knew he held the key to unravelling the tangled threads of deception woven around his family. The truth, though elusive, now beckoned him with a magnetic force.

His senses heightened, and Geoffrey exited the study as silently as he had entered. As he closed the door behind him, the weight of the newfound knowledge pressed against his chest. He was struck with the sudden desire to share this revelation with Lakshmi. He was thankful for the shadows of the nighttime, allowing him to sneak out of the main house easily. A few minutes later, he knocked at the door of Lakshmi's cottage.

The door creaked open slowly, and a sleepy-looking Lakshmi poked her head outside. Her eyes widened once they focused on his face.

"Geoffrey, what are you doing here at this time of the night?"

His grave expression didn't flicker. "May I come in?"

She blinked before opening the wider door for him to step through. The lamp's glow flickered inside the cottage, casting shadows in the room's corners.

"What brings you here so late!" Lakshmi asked, her voice was soft with both sleep and concern.

"Lakshmi," Geoffrey began, his voice a mix of urgency and resolution, "I found the letter in my father's study. It's from an anonymous sender – an Observer."

All the sleep left Lakshmi's face. Her eyes widened as she took in the gravity of the message. The words seemed to hang in the air, charged with the weight of revelation. "An Observer? This means someone deliberately framed me," she exclaimed, a spark of hope in her eyes.

Geoffrey nodded, sharing in her realization. "Yes, it suggests that someone had a hand in diverting attention to you. But the challenge is, we don't know who sent the letter. My father

CHAPTER 8   138

might have tried to find out, but we can't rely on that."

Lakshmi, undeterred by the uncertainty, met Geoffrey's gaze. "Geoffrey, this letter is a breakthrough. It means we're on the right track. Someone wanted to hide the truth, and now they've allowed us to uncover it."

Her hope was infectious, and Geoffrey found himself nodding along. "You're right, Lakshmi. We can't let this opportunity slip away. We need to act, but we must tread carefully. The guilty party might be watching."

Lakshmi, her mind already in motion, started to pace. "Let's start by discreetly talking to the servants. If the murderer is indeed among us, someone might know something. We have to gather information without alerting the guilty party."

Geoffrey nodded, acknowledging the wisdom in her words. "Agreed. We have to be cautious and thorough. If the culprit senses our pursuit, they might act hastily, and we can't afford that."

Lakshmi, her resolve unwavering, added, "We're getting closer, Geoffrey. Every step brings us nearer to the truth, one careful move at a time."

"Todd and I will look through my grandmother's study; perhaps we might be missing something too," Geoffrey said.

"Oh, Geoffrey. You broke into your father's study, didn't you?" Lakshmi asked, suddenly putting the dots together.

Trying to ignore the gravity of what he'd done, he shrugged. "It doesn't matter. I promised you I would help you regain your freedom." He was taken aback when Lakshmi closed the distance between them to hug him.

Her jasmine scent filled his senses. Geoffrey closed his eyes as his arms came to rest around her, too. He tried not to read too much into the hug, but despite his mental reassurances, his heart didn't stop leaping in his chest. Tonight, he'd given her hope, and she'd given him some in return.

CHAPTER 8   140

The grand mansion stood proudly amidst lush green gardens, its magnificence a testament to Lord Michael's wealth and power. As the sun began to set, the atmosphere seemed heavy with tension. Lord Michael nervously paced his room, and his mind was plagued with worry. He anxiously glanced out the window, expecting to see Geoffrey and Todd's figures on the horizon at any moment.

His loyal wife, Lady Grace, noticed his restlessness and stepped into the room, her elegant gown rustling softly against the floor. She looked at Lord Michael with surprise. "Michael, dear, what has gotten into you? You seem positively on edge."

Lord Michael sighed, his voice laden with anxiety. "Grace, Geoffrey is aligning himself with the servants, asking questions that he shouldn't be. I fear they may uncover secrets that are best left buried."

Lady Grace furrowed her brow, concern evident in her eyes. "Secrets? What secrets are you referring to, Michael? And why are you scared about Geoffrey searching for them?"

Lord Michael hesitated for a moment before gathering his thoughts. He had never confided in anyone about the truth behind Lady Michelle's tragic death. The burden had remained his alone to bear. But now, faced with the fear of exposure, he felt his anxiety bubbling to the surface.

"Grace, you've always been loyal to me," Lord Michael began, his voice trembling. "But there are dark things that I have hidden for far too long. Secrets that could ruin me if they ever came to light."

Lady Grace's eyes widened in alarm. "Michael, are you insinuating that you had a hand in Lady Michelle's death?"

Lord Michael's face contorted with anger, he snapped, "How dare you, Grace! I loved Lady Michelle with all my heart. Accusing me of such a heinous act is unforgivable!"

Surprised by her presumption, Lady Grace

CHAPTER 8   142

recoiled, realizing her mistake. "Michael, I apologize. I didn't mean to imply that you had any involvement in her passing. I only thought that perhaps your anxiety stemmed from fear of exposure."

Lord Michael's anger seemed to engulf him. "Expose what, Grace? What do you think I'm hiding? Why can't you trust that I am innocent?"

Lady Grace, filled with earnestness, reached out a hand to try and calm him down. "Michael, please, I didn't mean to upset you. I've always believed in your innocence. But the sudden fear you have expressed and the mention of secrets has shaken me."

Lord Michael's eyes blazed, his face turning red with anger. "Shaken you? Do you think I'm some villain hiding in plain sight? If my dear wife can't trust me, then who can?"

Lady Grace's voice quivered as she tried to regain her composure. "Michael, that's not what I meant. Please, let's not fight over this. We must stay united, especially now when the estate is scrutinised."

But Lord Michael, consumed by anger, would not be swayed. "United? How can we be united when you doubt me? I have always confided in you, Grace, but now you are questioning everything."

Tears rose in Lady Grace's eyes as she begged him to listen. "Michael, trust me, I never meant for it to come to this. I apologize from the depths of my heart. I should not have spoken without thinking, without realizing the pain it would cause you."

Lord Michael's anger slowly transformed into despair. His hand loosened its grip on the mantle, and he sank into a nearby chair, exhaustion etched into his features. "Grace, I appreciate your apology, but the damage has been done. I need time to clear my mind. I cannot bear this weight on my shoulders any longer."

Lady Grace extended her hand with a heavy

CHAPTER 8   144

heart, imploring him to reconsider. "Michael, please don't shut me out. I promise I will do whatever it takes to make amends and ease your burdens. We have been friends for too long, even before we got married, to let this tear us apart."

Lord Michael let out a bitter laugh. "Friends? Is that what we are now? I felt accused of a crime, Grace. Can you imagine the pain that brings? Our marriage might never recover from this."

His words hung in the air, heavy with regret and sorrow. Lady Grace's tears fell freely as she whispered, "No, Michael, please don't say that. I didn't mean to accuse you. I still believe in you."

But Lord Michael rose from his seat, his voice cold and distant. "I need some time alone, Grace. I cannot pretend that everything is fine when it isn't. Perhaps, in time, we will find a way to mend what has been broken."

Lord Michael stormed out of the room without

another word, leaving Lady Grace alone with her thoughts and the echoes of their heated argument. Her heart ached with loss as she realized that the bonds of their friendship had been tested like never before.

As the sun continued its descent, casting long shadows throughout the mansion, Lord Michael and Lady Grace were left to contemplate the aftermath of their heated exchange. This chasm seemed impossible to bridge. Time would tell whether their friendship, once so strong, could withstand the weight of secrets and mistrust.

Shortly after, Todd took a deep breath as he approached the grand entrance of Buckingham's Manor. The sprawling estate stood majestically before him, its manicured lawns and towering oak trees casting an imposing shadow. He tightened his grip on the handle of his suitcase, his excitement palpable as he anticipated seeing his friend, Geoffrey.

For hours, Todd had longed for a chance to talk to his newfound friend, to escape the

CHAPTER 8   146

monotony of his own life and embark on intriguing adventures alongside him. But fate seemed to be playing a cruel game, as each attempt to see Geoffrey had been thwarted by the overbearing nature of Lord Michael and Lady Grace, Geoffrey's parents.

Determined not to be discouraged, Todd walked briskly towards the carved oak doors adorned with intricate designs that whispered of wealth and power. As he reached out to knock, the doors swung open, revealing Lord Michael Buckingham, a towering figure of authority and unmistakable wealth. Todd felt a pang of nervousness, knowing he was about to face the stern judgment of Geoffrey's father.

"Good day, Master Todd," Lord Michael greeted curtly, his stern gaze piercing through Todd's soul.

"G-good day, sir," Todd stuttered, fighting to maintain his composure.

"What brings you here today? I hope it is not to burden my son with your whims and misadventures once again," Lord Michael huffed, his voice laced with irritation.

"N-no, sir. I only wished to see Geoffrey," Todd replied, his voice betraying his disappointment.

Lord Michael's brow furrowed. "You dare to influence my son with your recklessness and insolence? Geoffrey was never rude or disobedient until he befriended you and that criminal - Lakshmi."

Todd's heart sank at the accusation, feeling the weight of Lord Michael's disappointment pressing upon him. "I assure you, sir, I have only ever encouraged Geoffrey to explore the world around him. To experience life beyond these walls."

"And what good has that done him?" Lady Grace Buckingham interjected, her voice dripping with disdain as she joined her husband in the foyer. "Our son has become unruly, rebellious. It is because of your influence that he goes against our wishes."

CHAPTER 8   148

"I-I didn't mean for any harm, Lady Grace," Todd stammered, his eyes downcast to avoid their withering gaze. "I only seek to."

"That is not your place," Lord Michael declared, his tone final and unbending. "Geoffrey has been placed under house arrest for his disobedience. Your presence here is unnecessary and unwelcome. Return to your job while I let you keep it."

Todd flinched at the threat. He felt a swell of frustration rise within him, battling against the crestfallen disappointment that threatened to consume him whole.

"I understand, sir, Lady Grace," Todd said, his voice tinged with resignation. "If Geoffrey is not allowed to have visitors, I respect your decision. I will take my leave."

He turned on his heels, his footsteps heavy and slow as he exited Buckingham's Manor. The air was thick with silence, the weight of the missed opportunity hanging heavy on Todd's shoulders. His frustration morphed into a simmering anger as he walked away, his mind replaying the unfairness of it all.

How could Lord Michael and Lady Grace be so blind? Worse, how could they be callous to condemn Lakshmi so quickly? And now they tried to prevent the truth from being discovered by influencing Geoffrey.

As Todd trudged along the cobblestone path, his mind filled with bitterness and annoyance. He longed for a way to change the situation, to convince Geoffrey's parents of the error of their ways. But for now, he had no choice but to turn back and head to the servant's quarters, leaving behind the grandeur of Buckingham's Manor and the shattered fragments of his hopes.

The journey back seemed longer, his frustration and disappointment heavy upon his young shoulders. With each step, Todd's determination grew, fueled by a desire to prove himself, to show Lord Michael and Lady Grace that he was not the source of their son's disobedience. He would find a way to reach

CHAPTER 8   150

Geoffrey and help him, even if it meant going against the wishes of those in power.

Todd's resolve solidified as the sun sank below the horizon, casting a warm golden glow over the countryside. He would not be defeated. He would fight for his friendship, for Lakshmi and their newfound bond that had once connected him and Geoffrey. And with that determination fueling his every step, Todd trudged onward, ready to face whatever obstacles lay ahead.

As the sun began to set over their estate's vast, rolling hills, Lady Grace found herself in the garden, admiring the delicate petals of the blooming roses. Her thoughts, however, were far from the beauty surrounding her. It had barely been a day since Geoffrey, their only son, had returned from visiting Lakshmi and tensions between him and his father, Lord Michael, had been steadily escalating even with her.

Feeling a heavy burden upon her heart, Lady Grace resolved to confront her husband about their treatment of their son. She knew it was time to speak her mind and express her grave concerns. She sought out Lord Michael, finding him in his study, surrounded by stacks of books and bathed in the soft golden glow of candlelight. She took a deep breath, summoned her strength, and entered the room.

"Michael," she began, her voice adorned with compassion, "we must talk about Geoffrey."

Lord Michael looked up, his furrowed brows revealing the strains and worries that occupied his mind. A mixture of surprise and curiosity flickered in his eyes as he gestured for her to take a seat beside him.

"What troubles you, my love?" he asked, concern threading his words.

Lady Grace hesitated for a moment before choosing her words carefully. "I fear we are being too hard on Geoffrey, dear. It has been a few days since our row, and we've barely spoken to him."

Lord Michael's expression grew stern, his features etched with the weight of his

CHAPTER 8 152

responsibilities as a father. "Grace, our duty is to ensure Geoffrey grows into a disciplined and responsible young man. We cannot satisfy him forever."

"Yes, I understand that," Lady Grace interjected softly, resting her hand on his arm, "but we must also remember that he is still just a boy, craving our guidance and love. If we continue to push him away, we risk losing him entirely."

Lord Michael sighed deeply, his resolve seemingly unyielding. "Grace, I am merely teaching him the ways of the world, preparing him for the challenges that lie ahead. It is a necessary course of action."

"Perhaps," Lady Grace conceded gently, "but we should allow him to express his thoughts and feelings at least. We should truly listen to what he has to say."

Lord Michael considered his wife's words, a flicker of doubt momentarily crossing his face. "Very well," he relented, "we shall call a family meeting tomorrow evening."

Lady Grace's heart swelled with relief and gratitude, finally believing her voice had been heard. "Thank you, Michael. I believe this is a step in the right direction."

CHAPTER 8   154

CHAPTER 4

Somewhere in the future...

Lakshmi sat perched on a hillside overlooking the quaint and idyllic town, its vibrant houses adorned with colourful chipped paint. The cool breeze caressed her face, carrying the scent of freshly blooming jasmine flowers, infusing the air with tranquillity. As she gazed down at the town, nostalgia washed over her like waves crashing against the shore. It had been years since she had left, but the memories of her childhood here were etched deep within her heart.

The sun began its descent, casting a warm golden glow that painted the town in hues of amber and bronze. Lakshmi couldn't help but smile as she watched children playing in the narrow alleys below, their laughter like music echoing in the gentle winds. Their youthful energy was contagious, uplifting her spirits and filling her with joy.

As the children noticed her presence, they waved enthusiastically and called out to her, their voices carrying through the stillness of the evening. Lakshmi greeted each one with a fond smile, her eyes shining affectionately as they approached her.

"Namaste, Lakshmi Aunty!" a young girl named Riya exclaimed, her pigtails bouncing with every step. "Are you enjoying the view today?"

Lakshmi returned the greeting, her voice filled with warmth. "Namaste, Riya. Yes, I always find solace in this hillside, especially during twilight. It's a moment of tranquillity."

Riya's eyes twinkled with curiosity. "Aunty, what do you think of our town? Do you miss it when you're away?"

Lakshmi's smile grew wistful. "Oh, my dear, I miss this town every single day. The place holds a piece of my heart that can never be replaced. The memories, the friendships, and the essence of the people linger within me even when I'm

CHAPTER 8   156

far away."

The children gathered around Lakshmi, eager to hear her stories of yesteryears. She became their storyteller, painting vivid pictures of when the town buzzed with life and dreams flourished like the jasmine flowers that adorned the women's hair. As she spoke of family, love, and the simplicity of life, the children listened with wide-eyed wonder, trying to envision a world that seemed so distant yet enchanting.

As twilight deepened, the children started to disperse, bidding Lakshmi a fond farewell. Their parents' voices could be heard calling them home for dinner, and the serenity of the hillside was left undisturbed once more. Lakshmi remained seated, pensive, and reflective.

A group of teenagers, Hina, Anu, and Ravi, who had been observing from a distance, finally summoned the courage to approach Lakshmi. Hina, the most outspoken of the trio, initiated the conversation.

"Aunty, we have been coming here for days and watching you converse with the children. Your presence and wisdom intrigue us. Would you share your insights into the secrets of a harmonious family life?"

Lakshmi regarded the teenagers with wisdom gleaming in her eyes. "Family life, my dear ones, is like the strings of a sitar. Each string is unique, yet they intertwine to create a harmonious melody. It requires love, compassion, and understanding."

Anu's eyes sparkled as she interjected, "But, Aunty, how can we cultivate such a bond in this fast-paced world? It feels like everyone is running in different directions."

Lakshmi nodded, acknowledging the truth in Anu's words. "Indeed, the modern world demands navigation through countless distractions and responsibilities. But we must remember that true connection lies in the simplest gestures, moments of undivided attention and the willingness to listen truly."

CHAPTER 8   158

Ravi, the pensive one, sought further guidance. "Aunty, what about conflicts and differences within families? How do we handle those?"

Lakshmi's face softened as she spoke. "Conflict is inevitable, my dear Ravi. But how we approach and navigate these stormy waters defines the strength of our bonds. Allowing open communication, empathy, and compromise can bridge even the deepest chasms."

The teenagers absorbed Lakshmi's words, their minds expanding with newfound understanding. They stayed with her, engaging in a thoughtful conversation until the stars began to twinkle, one by one, in the inky sky. As the night embraced them, the teenagers bid farewell, promising to bring these seeds of wisdom into their lives.

Left alone once again, Lakshmi reflected upon the passing moments. She marvelled at the unyielding spirit of the town, a town where traditions and love still intertwined despite the encroachment of the modern age.

The following morning, Lakshmi sat in the comfort of her garden, surrounded by colourful flowers and the melodious chirping of birds. The warm afternoon sun caressed her face as she leaned back on her favourite wicker chair, a book resting gently on her lap. As she turned the pages absentmindedly, a messenger dressed in royal livery approached her.

"Excuse me, Lady Lakshmi," the messenger said, bowing respectfully. "I bring news from your younger sister, Meena." Lakshmi's eyes brightened with anticipation. Meena had given birth to her second child a few months ago, and Lakshmi eagerly awaited her sister's well-being and the new addition to their family. She thanked the messenger and eagerly took the letter.

As she unfolded the delicate parchment, her heart filled with joy. Meena's words vividly depicted their newborn niece, Radha, and the happiness that enveloped their household. Lakshmi's lips curled into a tender smile as she

CHAPTER 8   160

imagined the baby's tiny fingers and cooing voice.

Lost in her thoughts, once again, Lakshmi was startled by a man's voice that resonated from behind. "My dearest Lakshmi, I hope the news is as delightful as your smile suggests." Before she could react, the man had already wrapped his arms around her, pulling her into a warm embrace. Lakshmi turned around, her eyes meeting those of the man. His eyes twinkled with mischief, a characteristic trait that had attracted her to him since they both fell in love. "Come on!" she exclaimed, eliciting a hearty chuckle from the man. "You startled me!"

He kissed her forehead affectionately. "Apologies, my love. I couldn't resist sneaking up on you like old times." Lakshmi laughed, her worries momentarily forgotten. "It seems you haven't lost your mischievous touch, even after all these years." He cupped her face in his hands, gazing into her eyes with love. "And you, my dear, still have that sparkle which captivated my heart from the first moment I saw you." Their gazes lingered a moment longer, cherishing the love they'd shared for over a decade. But knowing Lakshmi's excitement, He couldn't hold back his curiosity any longer. "So, what brought that radiant smile to your face?"

Lakshmi handed him the letter from Meena, her eyes gleaming with joy. "Our dear Meena has given birth to another beautiful child. A daughter they named Radha. Just think, love, we have another little bundle of joy to shower with love." His eyes softened as he read the letter, a smile playing on his lips. "How wonderful! A daughter. Our niece, Radha. She will bring even more happiness to our family." Lakshmi nodded, her heart brimming with happiness. "Indeed, she will. We must visit soon and welcome the newest member of our family into this world."

"We shall," the man replied, pulling her closer. "But for now, let us cherish this moment, for we have so much to be grateful for." The world

CHAPTER 8 162

around them blurred into insignificance as they sat in their garden sanctuary, enveloped in each other's arms. Their love had endured the tests of time, and together, they had created a joyful life full of love and shared adventures.

Hours passed, and the crimson hues of dusk began to paint the sky when he finally broke the silence. "My love, the day is coming to a close. Shall we go inside and celebrate this wonderful news with a refreshing cup of tea?"

Lakshmi nodded, reluctantly pulling away from his embrace. As they strolled hand-in-hand toward their quaint cottage, they exchanged tales of their day, reminiscing about the memories they had created together. Inside the cosy kitchen, he prepared the tea while Lakshmi sat at the wooden table, still marvelling at the letter in her hands. The fresh aroma of tea leaves wafted through the air, mingling with the warmth of their love and joy.

He joined her at the table as he poured the tea into cups. His eyes sparkled with anticipation as he raised his cup, a toast to their expanding family. "To Meena, her husband, and little Radha – may their lives overflow with love and happiness." Lakshmi clinked her cup against his. Her voice was filled with gratefulness and love. "To family, togetherness, and the blessings that life brings. May our hearts always remain full." They sipped their tea, and their minds united in appreciation and affection. The news of Meena's baby had shared their world with hope and promise.

The moon shimmered over the tranquil hillside, casting a mesmerizing glow on the couple seated on the porch. Lakshmi's heart raced as she looked into her man's eyes, her emotions swirling like a tempest in her chest. The quiet evening was filled with anticipation, promising a night of intimacy yet unexplored.

Lakshmi's fingers lightly grazed the untouched glass of wine before her, her nervousness palpable. She stole glances at her companion, intrigued by how he effortlessly exuded charm

CHAPTER 8   164

and mystery. His presence alone sent shivers down her spine, igniting a fire that no words could describe.

As if sensing her restlessness, he extended his hand across the small distance between them, offering it as a beacon of reassurance. Lakshmi hesitated momentarily before intertwining her fingers with his, feeling an immediate surge of warmth course through her veins.

"I can't help but feel that we were destined to meet," Lakshmi murmured, her voice barely audible over the whispering breeze.

He smiled gently, his eyes conveying a depth of understanding that seemed to span lifetimes. "There are forces at work beyond our comprehension, Lakshmi. Perhaps the universe conspires to bring souls together when they need each other the most."

Lakshmi's heart fluttered at his words, her mind mesmerized by his enigmatic presence. The world felt suspended at that moment as if time had frozen to savour their connection.

CHAPTER 8 165

The conversation flowed effortlessly between them as if they had known each other all their lives. They spoke of dreams and aspirations, of shared passions and hidden desires. With each passing moment, they deepened their bond, nurturing an intimacy transcending the physical realm.

CHAPTER 8 166

The Present...

The dim lamplight cast flickering shadows on the wallpapered hallway as Geoffrey and Todd entered the seemingly endless maze of rooms. The air was heavy with a mixture of apprehension and curiosity as they sought clues that would shed light on the mysterious murder that had shaken Buckingham Manor. Geoffrey, a makeshift detective with furrowed brows, ran his gloved fingers along the dusty shelves in the first room they entered. The room seemed untouched for decades, with ancient furniture covered in white sheets, adding an eerie touch to the already sombre atmosphere.

Todd stepped behind Geoffrey. Although he lacked experience, his keen observation skills and determination made him a complementary partner to the makeshift detective. Todd followed Geoffrey's lead with a magnifying glass, ready to discover the secrets hidden within the mansion's unexplored walls. "Let's start with the Lady Michelle's study. If someone had murderous intent, they might have left behind something incriminating," Geoffrey suggested, his voice echoing in the empty room.

The door creaked open as they approached the study, revealing an opulent room filled with countless bookshelves and trinkets. The scent of aged leather and the faint perfume lingered in the air. Geoffrey halted in his steps.

"The study still smells like her." He said ruefully. Todd hesitantly hovered behind him, unsure whether to console him. The late Lady Michelle had been his grandmother, after all.

"She treasured her books a lot," Geoffrey said, breaking the awkward silence. He meticulously scanned each surface, admiring the impressive book collection on the shelves.

Todd, meanwhile, sifted through papers and opened drawers with care, searching for anything that might prove crucial to their investigation. Suddenly, Todd's face lit up excitedly as he held a worn leather-bound

CHAPTER 8   168

journal. "Geoffrey, look what I found! It seems to be a personal diary belonging to Lady Michelle.

Geoffrey's eyes widened, and the corners of his mouth turned upwards into a knowing smile. "Well done, Todd! Let's see if we can find any entries that could lead us closer to our murderer." They sat side by side in the elegant study, flickering by candlelight, engrossed in the secrets in the diary's pages. As they meticulously examined each entry, the tantalizing snippets of Lady Michelle's life began to take shape before their eyes.

"Listen to this," Geoffrey whispered, ensuring only Todd could hear him. "'April 15th, 1927. A strange encounter in the garden tonight. A hooded figure whispered ominous warnings in my ear, telling me to be wary of those closest to me. Could these words be mere drunken ramblings or a foreshadow of something sinister?'"

Todd's eyes gleamed with curiosity. "Who

could this hooded figure be? Could they have had something to do with the murder?" Geoffrey nodded thoughtfully. "Indeed, Todd. It seems Lady Michelle felt threatened by someone who knew her impending doom. We must find this hooded figure and unveil their true intentions."

With newfound determination, the duo continued their relentless search, moving from room to room, unravelling secrets concealed within the mansion's long-forgotten walls. Their quest for answers led them through dusty libraries, grand ballrooms, and hidden passages.

In a forgotten corner of the attic, among long-forgotten relics, they discovered a locked trunk, weathered by time. Geoffrey skillfully picked the lock, and its hinges creaked open to reveal a trove of letters tied with a fragile, yellowed ribbon. "These letters—look at the dates!" Todd exclaimed, holding one aloft. "All from different townspeople addressed to Lady Michelle. Some hint at secrets, others at

CHAPTER 8   170

resentment. Could one of these be our murderer?"

As they delved deeper into the attic's secrets, a gust of wind blew through the cracked window, sending papers flying in a frenzy around them. Geoffrey's eyes caught one particular letter that danced near his hand, and he snatched it from the air before it disappeared. "Listen, Todd," Geoffrey said, his voice almost a whisper. "'To Lady Michelle. The secrets you've hidden are no longer safe. Justice will be served, and your sins laid bare.'"

Todd's wide eyes met Geoffrey's gaze. "Who would send such a chilling message? And what secrets did Lady Michelle possess that someone would go to this extent to unveil?"

"It's a dead-end clue," Geoffrey said with a sigh. "There's no way we can find whoever wrote this letter. My grandmother had many enemies. As loved as she was, plenty of townsfolk didn't like how she ran the estate."

"At least this casts doubt on Lakshmi being the

sole suspect," Todd said, ever optimistic.

"I suppose. Come, I think it's high time we searched the other rooms in this house." Geoffrey walked out into the hallway.

The dimly lit corridor stretched ahead, with rows of closed doors on either side. Each door seemed to guard secrets within, waiting anxiously to be discovered. Adjusting the collars of their overcoats, Geoffrey and Todd exchanged a meaningful glance before embarking on their daunting task.

"Shall we start by searching through the rooms for any clues?" Todd suggested, breaking the eerie silence that had settled between them.

Geoffrey nodded in agreement. "Indeed, Todd. A thorough search may provide us with valuable information about the events leading up to the murder. Let's divide the work to make the process quicker. We'll keep turning over all the rooms till we find what we want."

With that, the two self-made investigators ventured into separate directions, Todd heading

CHAPTER 8 172

to the left wing while Geoffrey explored the right. The mansion was filled with an air of mystery, matched only by its opulence. In each room they entered, they were met with lavish furnishings, extravagant paintings, and antique curiosities, enough to impress anyone with a love for art and history. Yet, the tragedy that had unfolded overshadowed the grandeur of the mansion.

Todd entered the first room on his path, which appeared to be a study adorned with bookshelves and a mahogany desk. Hastening toward the arrangement of leather-bound volumes, he meticulously examined each book, hoping to find something unusual.

Meanwhile, Geoffrey found himself in a spacious bedroom which belonged to the deceased, filled with plush furniture and delicate chandeliers. The faint outline of a body, covered by a sheet, was still visible on the bed. With great care, Geoffrey shifted aside the bed sheet and knelt to examine the crime scene. His gloves gently explored the pockets of the bed, but there was nothing there but a small silver key.

As Geoffrey gently picked up the key from the side of the bed, he heard Todd's voice echoing through the corridor. "Geoffrey, you won't believe what I've found!"

Curiosity piqued, Geoffrey hurriedly made his way to the study. Todd stood in front of a particular shelf, his eyes fixated on a large antique book with intricate golden patterns etched on its spine.

"I stumbled upon this peculiar book, Geoffrey," Todd remarked, his excitement evident. "Look closely, it seems to be out of place."

Geoffrey examined the book carefully, noticing that it didn't seem to belong among the other volumes. Gingerly, he pulled the book from the shelf, revealing a hidden compartment. They found a stack of old letters, yellowed and fragile with age.

CHAPTER 8   174

"The letters must hold some significance," Geoffrey mused, his eyes scanning the delicate calligraphy on the aged parchment. "Let's take them back to Lakshmi for a closer examination with her."

Todd nodded in agreement, and they decided to continue their search for more clues before leaving the mansion. Stepping back into the hallway, they resumed their exploration, their minds racing to uncover the truth within the labyrinth of rooms.

Entering one room after another, they discovered a surprising pattern emerging. Many rooms seemed untouched, as if no one had set foot inside them for years. It became apparent that Lord Michael had deliberately kept certain areas of the mansion locked away, and Geoffrey theorized that the answers they sought might be hidden within one of these mysterious, restricted rooms.

"Now, listen here, Todd," Geoffrey whispered, "I am in command of this investigation. You will follow my lead, do you understand?"

Todd, a scruffy but intelligent man, responded with a smirk, "Oh, Geoffrey, always so eager to remind everyone who's in charge. I'll follow your lead, but don't expect me to kowtow to your every command."

Geoffrey scowled, his grip tightening on the magnifying glass he held. He was determined to put Todd in his place - all jokes. As they ventured deeper into the mansion, they entered a dimly lit corridor lined with locked doors. The air was heavy with an eerie silence, giving rise to the suspense in the atmosphere.

They started with the first room on the left, Geoffrey leading the way with Todd begrudgingly following. The room was filled with old paintings, dust-covered furniture, and forgotten memories. They moved methodically, inspecting every detail and searching for clues that might indicate the culprit responsible for the murder. Their banter commenced as they bent over to scrutinize an ornate photo frame.

CHAPTER 8   176

"You know, Geoffrey," Todd remarked, rolling his eyes, "You can't just assume authority solely based on your position. True leadership is earned, not demanded."

Geoffrey straightened up, his face red with anger. "I've earned my position through hard work and dedication, Todd! Unlike you, who seems to relish in defying my authority at every turn.

Todd arched an eyebrow, his patience wearing thin. "I've had enough of your high-handedness, Geoffrey. You may be my employer, but respect is a two-way street. I have valuable insights to offer, and I won't be sidelined. I'll search in this room whether you like it."

As they made their way through the unused master bedrooms, their footsteps echoed off the empty walls, creating an atmosphere of desolation and apprehension. The mansion seemed to hold its breath as if unwilling to reveal the secrets that lay within.

"If my company is so unpleasant, let's divide

CHAPTER 8 177

our search," Todd added.

Geoffrey scowled, but he was a little relieved. He quickly realised that Todd wasn't that bad; despite this, he did not intend to befriend him. "We'll cover more grounds that way."

As Todd explored the room methodically, Geoffrey kept a vigilant eye on his movements, and his anticipation tinged with irritation.

After thoroughly inspecting the room, Todd approached a set of ornate wooden chests nestled against the far wall. He pried one of the sturdy lids with careful precision, revealing a treasure trove of artefacts and long-forgotten keepsakes. His fingers brushed against a set of dusty bottles hidden in the corner, their contents mysterious and menacing.

"Geoffrey, come and look at this," Todd called out, his voice tinged with urgency. Suspecting that Todd had simply stumbled upon some trivial trinket, Geoffrey sauntered over reluctantly, his disdain evident.

"What is it now, Todd? More amateur

CHAPTER 8 178

sleuthing?" Geoffrey sneered, the tension between them simmering just below the surface.

Todd held up the dusty bottles, his expression grave. "These are no ordinary bottles, Geoffrey. They contain poisons, carefully concealed and hidden away. "

Geoffrey's initial scepticism gave way to shock and concern as he inspected the contents of the bottles. The implications of Todd's discovery were chilling, and the realization that someone within the mansion had planned Lady Michelle's demise weighed heavily on both men.

Their rivalry momentarily forgotten, they joined forces in a shared determination to unravel the sinister machinations that had led to the murder. The discovery of the hidden poison bottles signified a turning point in their investigation, propelling them to delve deeper into the dark underbelly of the mansion and its inhabitants.

"I knew it," Geoffrey said, but there was no

echo of triumph in his voice. "Whoever killed Lady Michelle is a member of this household, the killer is indeed amongst us."

CHAPTER 8 180

CHAPTER 5

It had been a whole year since Lakshmi left her hometown, embarking on a journey to discover herself and carve a new path in life. Her life at Buckingham Manor had been filled with ups and downs—more downs than ups in recent times—she'd made plenty of friends and learned so much. Yet, her heart still ached for the family she left behind, hoping they would understand her reasons for leaving someday.

She was pleasantly surprised to receive a package from her family that day. She hadn't thought they were counting the days as she had. Her heart thudded a fast beat in excitement as she opened the box. It was filled to the brim with goodies—a hand-knit scarf, a collection of herbal teas, a small journal with intricate patterns, and a pocket-sized painting kit. Each item seemed to whisper promises of forgotten joys and new beginnings.

Lost in the sea of excitement, Lakshmi

momentarily forgot the burdens she carried and allowed herself to indulge in the simple pleasures before her. She reached for the painting kit and began to dip her brush into vibrant colours, watching as they danced across the canvas, creating their own world. The act of creation felt liberating as if she could visualize her dreams coming to life.

As hours melted into minutes, Lakshmi's exhilaration faded into tranquillity. She then decided to prepare a cup of herbal tea, hoping its soothing properties would help her find solace amidst the chaos she was currently facing. But just as she was about to pour the boiling water over the tea bag, a familiar, authoritative voice echoed through the cottage.

"Lakshmi! How dare you indulge in such frivolities!"

Startled, Lakshmi turned around and faced her Madame, Lady Grace, standing in the doorway with an expression of disdain on her face. Lakshmi's heart sank at that moment, and she

CHAPTER 8   182

felt like the heavens had conspired against her.

"I cannot believe you dare to enjoy yourself when you have subjected our family to so much pain!" Lady Grace's voice trembled angrily, her icy words piercing the air.

Lakshmi stood frozen, her hands clutching the delicate porcelain teacup, as Lady Grace stormed towards her, snatching the cup away.

"You have no right to happiness, Lakshmi, not after what you selfishly put us through," Lady Grace seethed. Her eyes bore into Lakshmi's, filled with fury and anguish.

Lakshmi's heart shattered into a million pieces at the sight of Lady Grace's pain. She had always hoped that Lady Grace and the family would come to understand her need for self-discovery and hoped for justice by how, but she had never anticipated the magnitude of their resentment.

"I never intended to cause you pain, my lady," Lakshmi whispered, her voice laced with remorse. "Leaving my home was the hardest decision ever, but I needed to find myself. I needed to live a life that was true to my desires, and I thought this was the best way to do it. I never had any intentions of hurting anyone."

Lady Grace's features softened slightly, her anger momentarily replaced by confusion. "But at what cost, Lakshmi? Our family suffered upon your arrival. Lady Michelle died, Lord Michael lost his spirit, and my dear Geoffrey... he missed you every day you were behind bars and has almost driven himself crazy just because he feels he needs to clear your name. Are you some cancer?"

Tears welled up in Lakshmi's eyes, mirroring the pain across Lady Grace's face. "I never wanted to cause them any pain. I never thought my presence would suffocate people who can make my dreams come true."

Lady Grace sighed, feeling the weight of the situation unfold between them. "Lakshmi, you might have left to follow your dreams. But what about the dreams you are shattering? Our

CHAPTER 8   184

dreams of seeing our son settle down, create a family, and bring joy to our household? While his parents grow old together."

Lakshmi's shoulders slumped, her guilt threatening to overpower her. "I understand your disappointment, Grace. And I'm sorry for the pain I've caused. But I didn't bear the thought of living a life that felt suffocating to people around me. I had to find my path, even if it meant hurting anyone. I left my family knowing they'd greatly miss me, but I had. Moreover, I didn't harm your family intentionally."

As silence enveloped the room, Lady Grace's features remained stubbornly stony. "I don't like what you bring to my family, and I can't watch you keep tearing my family apart." Without warning, she snatched the box from Lakshmi's grip.

With a startled cry, Lakshmi let go. "My lady..."

"You seem to have forgotten your place here.

You're a prisoner here, and you'll pay for your crimes against this family." Lady Grace spat. With that, she spun on her heels and left the room. Lakshmi dared not let the tears fall until the door slammed shut.

The door creaked open, and Geoffrey and Todd walked in. Lakshmi wasn't surprised to see them together, but both continued to deny the friendship blooming and disguised it under camaraderie. Now, Todd wore a look of concern on his face, identical to the furrow of Geoffrey's face tinged with shame. If only he knew that Lakshmi didn't grudge him for his family's treatment of her.

"Lakshmi, we heard what happened," Todd said.

"I can't believe my mother would be so awful," Geoffrey said gruffly.

Lakshmi forced a smile. "It's not her fault. She's doing what she thinks is best for her family."

Geoffrey shook his head. "She knows who you

CHAPTER 8   186

are. She once treated you like her own daughter. How could her opinion change so fast?"

"Geoffrey, it's all right." Lakshmi insisted. The last thing she wanted was for Geoffrey to alienate his family further because of her. Although Lady Grace's actions hurt her deeply, she didn't want any more trouble.

"It's not all right." It was Todd who spoke. "Which is why we're here to fix it." His smile was borderline mischievous. "We're going to steal your package back.

Lakshmi's eyes widened in surprise. "Steal? You can't..." She looked at Geoffrey. "Tell Todd that this plan is not worth it."

Geoffrey shrugged. "We understand the risks, Lakshmi, but we believe it is worth it."

Lakshmi was torn. On one hand, their offer showcased an unparalleled and selfless devotion to her. But on the other, she couldn't bear the thought of them getting into trouble for her sake. Still, her heart yearned for things to return to how they were before; perhaps this was the only way to achieve it.

"Geoffrey, Todd, I truly appreciate your loyalty and bravery, but I cannot let you endanger yourselves for me," Lakshmi said, her voice filled with genuine concern.

Todd reached out, placing a hand on Lakshmi's shoulder. "Lakshmi, we are adults capable of making our own choices. We've weighed the consequences and decided that, whatever happens, it will be worth it to see you smile again."

She looked hesitantly at Geoffrey. "I can't take it. Your mother will notice if it goes missing."

Geoffrey shrugged. "I'll take the fall for it then." Sensing her hesitance, he added, "Please, let us do this one thing for you, Lakshmi."

It was the softness of his voice that undid her resolve. Lakshmi found herself nodding in agreement.

Lakshmi's gratitude for her friends swelled within her. Their unwavering support melted away her reservations, and with a nod, she

CHAPTER 8   188

silently agreed to the plan.

Determined, the trio began discussing the details of their audacious endeavour.

Elsewhere, in the bustling city of Wallington, Lady Grace found herself navigating through the labyrinthine streets. A determined stride replaced her usual elegant poise, her eyes scanning the buildings purposefully. A brass plaque caught her attention as she turned a corner: "Hastings & Associates - Lawyers and Consultants."

Curiosity tugged at Lady Grace's insatiable desire for knowledge and exploration. Without a second thought, she stepped into the office and was immediately greeted by a middle-aged man with thick-rimmed glasses perched on his nose. "Good evening, Lady Grace. I've been expecting you." The lawyer rose to his feet to greet her.

He ushered her into his office eagerly. It wasn't every day that one had the opportunity to serve the Buckingham family.

CHAPTER 8 189

"A dear friend recommended your service, Mr. Hastings. I find myself intrigued by the possibilities within your establishment," she replied, offering a polite smile. "Might we engage in a conversation about various business ideas?"

The lawyer, Mr. Hastings, gestured towards a plush armchair in his office. Lady Grace settled into the seat, her eyes sparkling with anticipation and ideas swirling in her mind. Mr Hastings sat behind his desk; curiosity mirrored in his eyes as he studied the unconventional visitor before him.

"Tell me, Lady Grace, what business ideas have piqued your interest?" Mr. Hastings asked, leaning forward attentively.

"My family's estates have suffered in recent times. We could blame it on years of reckless indulgence by my husband. My mother-in-law tried her best to restore Buckingham Manor, but her methods were a little outdated, for a lack of better words..." Lady Grace trailed off. "I want

CHAPTER 8   190

to change our fortune, Mr. Hastings. And I intend to do whatever it takes."

Mr. Hastings listened intently, making notes on a legal pad as Lady Grace passionately detailed her plans. He nodded occasionally, but he barely spoke a word.

As the discussion neared, a sense of urgency hung in the air. Lady Grace leaned forward, her voice filled with determination. "Mr. Hastings, I want Buckingham Manor to be successful, no matter the cost. If necessary, I will bend the rules to ensure that happens."

Mr. Hastings arched an eyebrow, studying Lady Grace with a keen gaze. He understood the depth of her ambition, her hunger for success. But there was something about her words that left a chilling uneasiness hanging in the room.

"Lady Grace," he began cautiously, "while I appreciate your enthusiasm, I must remind you that laws and regulations must be obeyed. Crossing those lines could lead to dire consequences."

CHAPTER 8   191

For the longest moment, she was quiet, her lips pursed as if she was contemplating her words before she spoke them. The tick-tock of the grandfather clock filled the room and the lawyer held his breath as he awaited her answer.

A smile spread on her lips, her eyes glinting with a mix of determination and secrecy. "Mr. Hastings, there are always ways around those laws. It's just a matter of finding the right path to success.□

CHAPTER 8   192

CHAPTER 6

The first obstacle was gaining access to Lady Grace's room. This, combined with Todd's nimble fingers and knack for lock picking, seemed to provide a promising chance of success. Under the cloak of night, Geoffrey and Todd made their way to Lady Grace's estate wing. The moonlight bathed the corridors in an ethereal glow as they carefully manoeuvred through the dimly lit passageways, their hearts pounding with anticipation and trepidation.

Finally, they reached Lady Grace's door. With steady hands, Todd inserted the lock pick, deftly manipulating the tumblers until he heard a satisfying click. The door swung open silently, revealing Lady Grace's opulent chamber, filled with priceless antiques and elegant furnishings.

Todd and Geoffrey stood together in Lady Grace's room, their hearts pounding. Lakshmi's box sat on the nightstand beside the bed. Geoffrey grabbed it and jerked his head in a nod at Todd. Their work here was done. Despite his earlier nonchalance, he felt a little unsettled about breaking into his mother's room.

"Let's go." He whispered to Todd.

However, something caught Todd's attention amidst the opulence—a small corner, dimly lit and almost hidden from view. His curiosity piqued, and he walked over to investigate, Geoffrey following closely behind. To their shock, they discovered a hidden stash of bottles, neatly arranged and filled with a white powdery substance. Todd's eyes widened as he recognized the deadly compound—arsenic. He turned to Geoffrey, his voice full of concern.

"Geoffrey, do you see what I see?" Todd asked, his voice barely above a whisper.

Geoffrey's eyebrows furrowed as he nodded, picking up one of the bottles and examining it with curiosity and unease.

"It's the same bottle found in Lakshmi's room," Todd added. "Why are there several bottles of it in your mother's—" his words were

CHAPTER 8   194

cut short as realization dawned on him. Todd's eyes widened. "Your mother—Lady Grace killed Lady Michelle."

Geoffrey was silent. He, too, had come to the same staggering realization. His face was ashen, and he couldn't meet Todd's eyes.

Just as Todd was about to suggest their next move, a chilling voice interrupted their thoughts. "What do you think you're doing with that arsenic?" the voice demanded.

Todd and Geoffrey froze, slowly turning to face the ominous figure standing in the doorway. Lord Michael, Lady Grace's husband and Geoffrey's father had returned unexpectedly from his journey in India. His eyes darted between the two men, his gaze filled with suspicion and malice.

Lord Michael stepped forward, his voice dripping with venom. "Explain yourselves! Why are you snooping around my wife's room?"

Stammering, Todd managed to find his voice, holding up the bottle as evidence. "We found these bottles of arsenic hidden away in this room, my lord. We believe someone in this house has been using it."

Lord Michael's face paled, a mixture of panic and anger flashing across his features. He quickly composed himself, a cold smile forming on his lips. "You misunderstand, Todd. Lady Grace was a woman of great taste, and she collected rare artefacts. This, unfortunately, is one of them."

Todd exchanged a sceptical glance with Geoffrey, but before he could voice his doubts, Lord Michael stepped closer, his voice low and full of menace. "If you know what's good for you, you will keep this discovery to yourselves. The reputation of our family must remain untarnished. A Lady accused of murder would bring disgrace upon our name."

Todd's protests died on his lips as Lord Michael's words silenced him. The threat and power emanating from him were enough to make Todd tremble. Fear mingled with

CHAPTER 8   196

confusion as he desperately looked to Geoffrey for support, hoping he would see reason and stand by his side.

To his dismay, Geoffrey's face grew cold, his eyes filled with resignation. He took a step back, lowering his gaze. "Father, perhaps you're right. We should keep this quiet for the sake of our family."

The words struck Todd like a dagger to the heart. The bond he had thought he shared with Geoffrey shattered in an instant. Betrayal surged through his veins, mixing with his anger and confusion. He clenched his fists, his voice quivering with hurt and determination.

"I can't believe what I'm hearing, Geoffrey. We can't let someone get away with murder just because of their status! This is wrong!"

Lord Michael's face hardened further as he interjected, his voice laced with menace. "You'd better reconsider your words, Todd. Remember who holds the power in this household. If you breathe a word of this discovery to anyone, not only will Lady Grace be ruined, but you too will face dire consequences."

Todd's heart raced, torn between his desire for justice and the real fear for his safety. He knew he had to tread carefully, but the fire inside him refused to be extinguished. He locked eyes with Geoffrey one last time, searching for any flicker of the loyalty they had once shared, but found nothing.

In a cloud of anger and confusion, Todd turned his back on the two men. His shattered trust burdened him as he stormed out of the room and down the grand staircase. Still, he vowed to uncover the truth and fight against the injustices occurring within the estate's walls. The road ahead may be treacherous, but Todd was determined to carry the burden of truth, even if he had to do it alone.

Elsewhere, in the heart of London, the elegant figure of Lady Grace stepped out of the sombre-looking lawyer's office. Her emerald-green eyes were brimming with determination and a touch

CHAPTER 8   198

of desperation. The weight of her family's crumbling fortune burdened her every step as she walked briskly down the bustling streets.

The dark clouds overhead mirrored her sombre mood, casting an oppressive shadow over her as she hailed a carriage. She had just received news that her family's home, which she has spent the last few years protecting, a sprawling estate in the countryside, was at risk of being foreclosed. Lady Grace knew that time was of the essence, and she couldn't afford a moment's delay.

As she climbed inside the plush carriage, her heart raced with anxiety. She pulled her dark cloak tighter around her shoulders, shielding herself from the chill of the outside world. Frustration boiled within her as she barked at the carriage driver, her voice quivering with urgency.

"Faster, James! We must reach my family home as quickly as possible. Every minute counts!"

James, a middle-aged man with greying hair and kind eyes, nodded in acknowledgement, lovingly patting the side of the carriage. "Aye, my lady. We shall not waste a moment more." He was well aware of the predicament Lady Grace faced, for the rumours of her family's financial troubles had spread through the town like wildfire. Though he worried for her well-being, he knew better than to question her orders. The carriage lurched forward, its wheels clattering against the cobblestones as it darted through the crowded streets.

As the carriage raced towards the city's edge, Lady Grace's mind swirled with memories of her once glorious family. They had held a prestigious place in society, their wealth and influence matching their impeccable lineage. But as the years passed, her husband's profligate spending and failed investments had left them on the brink of ruin.

Grace's determination grew stronger with every thud of the horse's hooves. She inherited

CHAPTER 8   200

her mother's unwavering resilience and refused to allow her family's name to fade into obscurity. She clenched her fists, her knuckles white with the strain as she contemplated her next move.

The carriage rattled to a halt outside the imposing wrought-iron gates that guarded her family's home. The grand manor stood tall and imposing against the backdrop of the rolling hills. She could almost hear the echo of her ancestors' grandiose laughter drifting on the wind. But now, its once-vibrant halls rang hollow with the stain of their misfortunes.

Grace rushed out of the carriage, her skirts swirling around her feet as she pushed open the heavy doors. In her haste, she did not heed the cobwebs clinging to the chandeliers or the thick layer of dust that coated every surface. This was her battle to fight, and she would not let the past deter her.

As Lady Grace strode through the empty corridors, each step reverberated through the hollow house. She entered the study, where her husband had spent countless hours poring over ledgers and making ill-fated decisions. Grace's gaze fell upon a painting of her mother, which she had done after her mom's funeral. She was a serene woman with a kind smile, her emerald eyes mirroring Grace's own.

Her resolve strengthened, and Grace slumped into her husband's worn leather chair. She opened a drawer and withdrew a weathered document—a potential solution to their impending foreclosure. She had struck an agreement with an influential businessman, Mr. Harrington, who had expressed interest in purchasing portions of the estate's vast lands.

Lady Grace signed the document tremblingly, accepting the deal to grant her the funds needed to keep their family home intact. She clutched the paper tightly as though its mere presence could breathe life back into her family's fortune. But deep within, she knew that this was a temporary remedy. The path ahead was laden

CHAPTER 8   202

with challenges and sacrifices.

Grace's hands clenched, and a fire ignited within her. She would not rest until her family stood proud again, regaining their place in society's elite. A surge of determination coursed through her veins, dispelling her fears and replacing them with a steely resolve.

As she left the study, Lady Grace heard the distant sound of horse hooves approaching. A messenger had arrived with a letter containing news of her husband's unexpected investment turnaround. A glimmer of hope danced in her eyes, evident even in the dim light of the hallway.

*****

Later in the evening, the moon sat high in the inky black sky as Geoffrey stumbled out of the tavern, his mind clouded by the numbing effects of alcohol. His steps were unsteady, and he weaved through the deserted streets, swaying as if the ground beneath him was a tempestuous sea.

CHAPTER 8   203

As he stumbled along, a foggy determination settled upon Geoffrey's intoxicated mind. It had been a while since he had any serious conversation with his mother, filled with unanswered questions and the bitter taste of being left out of secrets. Something deep within him urged him to seek her out, to confront her and demand the truth. Truth, he thought bitterly, was a fleeting and elusive mistress.

His intoxicated thoughts turned to head to his mother's room in the grand estate nestled in the rolling hills of the countryside. His foggy memories whispered of a place he hadn't set foot in since he was caught with Todd by his father. "That's where she'll be," he whispered to no one in particular, his voice slurring.

With a sudden burst of determination, Geoffrey staggered towards the stables, his bleary eyes searching for a means of transportation. And then he saw an elegant black horse glistening like a shadow against the moonlit night. A bold idea ignited within him,

CHAPTER 8   204

fueled by liquid courage and overwhelming emotions.

In a moment of madness, he climbed clumsily onto the horse's back, gripping the reins tightly as the animal stirred beneath him. He kicked his heel into its side, urging it forward without a destination. The horse, startled by the sudden intrusion, galloped off into the night, carrying Geoffrey towards the haunting memories of his past.

The wind howled through Geoffrey's hair, slapping against his face, as he approached the familiar iron gates leading to his mother's family home. The estate's grandeur loomed before him like a brooding giant amidst the darkness. The horse clattered to a stop at the entrance, shaking its head in protest.

Geoffrey dismounted clumsily, landing heavily on the gravel below. His legs wobbled beneath him, and a wave of dizziness washed over him as he approached the towering front door. With a mix of trepidation and an alcohol-fueled sense of righteousness, he pounded his fist against the wood, demanding entrance into the fortress of his past.

The door creaked open slowly, revealing the dishevelled figure of his mother before him. Her eyes widened in shock as she took in the sight of Geoffrey, swaying unsteadily on the threshold. Her voice trembled with apprehension as she spoke, "Geoffrey? How did you find your way here? I thought we wouldn't get a word together again."

Ignoring her question, Geoffrey pushed past his mother, stumbling through the exquisitely decorated hallway. Hatred and resentment fueled his every movement. The world around him spun in a blur, the grandeur of the ancestral home mocking him as he made his way towards the truth that had eluded him for so long.

His mother followed closely behind, her hands reaching out to steady him. "Geoffrey, please," she implored, her voice tinged with desperation. "Let's talk. It would help if you didn't come

CHAPTER 8   206

home like this. You're drunk."

"No," Geoffrey slurred defiantly, his anger boiling over. "You left! You left me... you left me with no explanation, and I want to know why! Why did you not say a thing to me? I know you poisoned Lady Michelle."

Lady Grace gasped. Her eyes darted around the darkness as if she feared someone would hear. "I did it for your father, for you. Lady Michelle was going to disinherit him!"

The force of the truth caused Geoffrey to flinch.

His mother's face contorted with pain, her eyes brimming with tears. "Geoffrey, it's not that simple," she whispered, her voice cracking. "There were reasons, things you wouldn't understand."

"I can't understand because I don't know!" Geoffrey yelled, his voice echoing through the empty corridors. "Tell me the truth, damn it!"

"I did the best I could, Geoffrey," she pleaded, her voice cracking under her regret. "Your father's debts and behaviours, Lady Michelle's death, we're all out of my hands. I had to do what was best for you." Something within Geoffrey snapped. The anger simmering below the surface suddenly erupted into a volcano of rage.

As she turned to leave, her breath hitching with the weight of her unspoken words, Geoffrey lunged forward, gripping her arm in a drunken haze. The sudden movement caused her to lose balance, and with a terrible cry, she stumbled backwards towards an open balcony door.

He seemed too slow as Geoffrey watched his mother teeter on the edge, her arms flailing helplessly in mid-air. Panic flooded his veins as he realized the gravity of the situation, but his intoxication rendered him incapable of preventing the tragedy that was about to unfold.

With a sickening thud, his mother's body hit the ground, lifeless and broken. The impact seemed to jar the reality back into Geoffrey's hazy mind, and he crumbled to the floor, his

CHAPTER 8   208

legs unable to support his weight any longer. The room spun around him, his insides churning with a mix of grief and regret.

*****

The morning, it dawned upon the grand estate of Lord Michael with a heavy air of sorrow and despair. The usually bustling servants moved about with quiet solemnity, exchanging whispers and sympathetic glances. The once vibrant manor now stood shrouded in a cloud of grief as the news of Lady Grace's untimely demise spread like wildfire.

It was a crisp Tuesday morning, the momentous day that was destined to change the course of many lives forever. While the sombre ambience lingered in every nook and cranny of the estate, the noise of the approaching carriage broke the silence. Out stepped James, the carriage driver, his face lined with sorrow and grief.

With weary eyes, James approached the front steps of the manor and was met by Todd.

CHAPTER 8   209

Todd's heart sank as he examined the crestfallen expression on James's face.

"Tell me it is not true," Todd pleaded, his voice quivering with trepidation.

James nodded solemnly, his sorrowful voice laced, "I'm afraid it is, Todd. Lady Grace has passed away in the night. Lord Michael is devastated."

Todd leaned against the stone pillar of the entrance, his body and mind consumed by a whirlwind of emotions. Nobody else did, but he knew what Lady Grace had done, how she'd murdered her mother-in-law and framed Lakshmi for it. Now, she was dead.

As the news of Lady Grace's death sunk deeper into Todd's consciousness, another piece of information pierced through the haze of his thoughts. Geoffrey, the treacherous son responsible for Lady Grace's condition, had been apprehended by the authorities. It seemed that he had cracked under the weight of his guilt and confessed his heinous acts, leading to his

CHAPTER 8   210

arrest.

A glimmer of hope emerged in Todd's heart. Perhaps with Geoffrey's confession, the truth would finally prevail, and justice would be served. Todd's eyes narrowed with determination as he clutched tightly onto a crumpled envelope in his pocket—the evidence he had gathered against Lady Grace, which he had discreetly sent to the police.

This evidence would ensure Geoffrey's conviction and, ultimately, Lakshmi's freedom. Days turned into weeks, and the wheels of justice slowly began to turn. Todd eagerly awaited news of the progress of Geoffrey's trial, praying that it would be the key to Lakshmi's liberation. Weeks stretched into months, and just as despair threatened to consume him entirely, a piece of news reached Todd's ears.

"Lakshmi has been freed!" Lord Michael's voice echoed through the manor.

Relief washed over Todd as he was grateful for fate's unexpected twists. The truth had been unveiled, and Lakshmi was finally vindicated. Consumed by guilt for not recognizing Geoffrey's malicious intentions, Lord Michael decided to compensate Lakshmi generously. A sum that far exceeded her dreams of salvation.

The weight of guilt lay heavily upon Lord Michael's shoulders. He, too, had been deceived by Geoffrey's charming facade, which had cost his beloved wife's life. Determined to make amends, Lord Michael turned his attention to Lakshmi. No amount of money could ever bring Lady Michelle back, but perhaps it could help start anew for this innocent soul. He approached her with a new offer.

"Lakshmi," he began, his voice laced with regret, "I cannot undo the past, but I can try to make amends. As a token of my remorse, I am offering you considerable compensation. Take it and return to your homeland, back to Kerala."

This unexpected turn of events took aback Lakshmi. She had never anticipated such a gesture from Lord Michael, let alone the thought

CHAPTER 8   212

of returning to India. But the weight of England's beautiful and painful memories was becoming unbearable. She longed for the comfort and familiarity of her homeland. And after much contemplation, she made her decision.

"Yes, Lord Michael. I shall accept your offer," Lakshmi replied, her voice steady despite the jumble of emotions within her. "I will take the next ship back to Kerala."

Days turned into weeks, and Lord Michael's generous compensation opened up a realm of possibilities for Lakshmi. Amidst mixed emotions of gratitude and melancholy, Lakshmi made the difficult decision to return to her homeland in Kerala. She longed for the warmth of familiarity, the loving embrace of her family, and the solace of her ancestral home.

While packing her belongings, Lakshmi stood before Todd one last time. The air crackled with a bittersweet intensity as they gazed into each other's eyes, knowing their time together had

CHAPTER 8 213

ended. The knowledge of their imminent separation weighed heavily upon their hearts.

"I cannot express the depth of my gratitude, Todd," Lakshmi whispered, her emotion-filled voice. "Without your unwavering support, I would have been forever trapped in a web of lies and deceit."

Todd smiled softly, his eyes betraying a deep longing, "You deserve every ounce of justice, Lakshmi. I am glad to have played my part in setting things right."

She placed her hand tenderly on his heart, feeling its steady rhythm beneath her palm. She swallowed as her eyes met his.

In the quiet solitude of the orchard, Lakshmi and Todd found solace in each other's arms. They knew their time together was fleeting, but the memory of that night would forever be etched in their souls. In the depth of their emotions, they made love.

As the sun rose over the English countryside, Lakshmi sat alone in her room, lost in her

CHAPTER 8 214

thoughts. She had spent months in this foreign land, hoping to start a new life with Geoffrey by her side. But now, the unexpected events had shattered her dreams and left her heartbroken.

At this point, Lakshmi knew Todd was the only one she had truly loved and would have loved for them to be together, but she was scared of telling him to come with her to Kerala, not knowing how he'd react. There was no future for the two of them, not after everything that had happened. A heaviness weighed on Lakshmi's chest as she considered her next steps. She realized that the life she had built for herself in England had crumbled in just one fateful night. But amidst the ruins, there was a glimmer of hope. The evidence had exonerated her from all accusations, and she was now a free woman.

When the first rays of sunlight pierced through the morning mist, Lakshmi knew the time had come. With a heavy heart and packed belongings, she bid farewell to Todd, her

CHAPTER 8 215

confidant, protector, and lover.

"Goodbye, Todd," Lakshmi whispered, her voice choked with tears. "As long as I live, you'll always be in my heart."

CHAPTER 8   216

CHAPTER 7

Lakshmi still couldn't believe she was leaving England, even while she stood by the pier and watched the gulls fly, their piercing screams filling the air, their wings flapping against their slender white bodies. She lowered her gaze and eyed the vessels absently, taking in their hypnotic swaying forms on the water, her mind slowly detaching from the present and travelling to the recent past and the ordeal she had experienced in the hands of those she had thought were family.

The Buckinghams, she thought bitterly. What a harrowing experience she had had. It seemed like a dream. No. A nightmare. One that she had fortunately woken up from but had not done so unscathed. She had the physical scars to remind her if she dared to forget. She had come to England with an open mind, excited and ready for the new world ahead of her. Then, disaster sought her out and found her, drastically turning her life into a catastrophic mess. A part of her felt very numb, as though it was simply a witness to everything and nothing more, a phantom attached to herself, hovering above and watching with an odd sort of detachment Lakshmi couldn't explain nor understand. While she marvelled about that, she was much more aware of the other part of her, which felt such an intense hatred and resentment for all the people who had wronged her.

Accused of murder, locked up in prison, faced humiliation like she had never experienced. It had seemed as though her travails were never going to end. But then her luck had turned, the little of it that was left. She was finally going back to Kerala. The thought brought hot tears to her eyes, and she blinked and took several breaths to steady herself. She had to pull herself together, now more than ever. Crying over all that happened did nothing to change the past. All she could do was put that cursed family and the wickedness associated with its members

CHAPTER 8   218

behind her.

Todd, she thought fondly. That was one person she would never forget. Todd had been her rock, even while she was languishing in that filthy place she didn't want to remember. She was going to miss him. She thought she could still smell the fragrances on her skin, a reminder of the night she had spent with him in the orchard amongst the flowers and sweet-smelling leaves. That was one memory she would cherish, a rope to pull her out of the darkness of her thoughts whenever she got in too deep. It was sad that she could not stay, even with Todd. Her life in England was over. Any memories she hoped to make would be soiled by her experiences and the knowledge that the Buckinghams were not far off. Kerala beckoned to her. Her hometown is where she hoped to get healing.

She had no doubt her family would accept her, no matter the stories they had heard about her from Lord Michael. She would tell them all that had transpired during her stay in England with

CHAPTER 8 219

the Buckinghams, especially from her own perspective. And then she would leave them to judge if she deserved the treatment she had received at the hands of Lord Michael, his wife and his son, Geoffrey, who was more like his father now that Lakshmi thought about it. The apple didn't fall far from the tree in their case.

Lakshmi tamped down the bitterness she could feel rising in her chest. All of it was in the past now. She took a deep breath and closed her eyes, imagining for a second that she was pulling all the unpleasant memories and experiences into that one breath; then she let it out slowly until she felt as light as air inside. The sound of the foghorn pulled her from her brief moment of respite. She opened her eyes and made for the ship, mindful of the limp she knew she would have for the remainder of her life. One more thing to thank the Buckinghams for.

The trip back to India was going to be extended. Lakshmi faintly remembered the

CHAPTER 8   220

journey that brought her to England and how arduous it was. She was a young girl then, innocent and inexperienced to the wickedness man could perpetrate. She was a grown woman now, filled with knowledge she had gleaned in the harshest of ways. It had changed her. But to what extent?

With polite smiles, Lakshmi climbed aboard along with the other passengers, men and women. One good thing Lord Michael's 'compensation' had done was buy her an expensive ticket for the journey, so it didn't shock her to see the calibre of people she was travelling with. It was a merchant ship but of a higher class. And there were passengers as well as cargo. The passengers were the rich and the wealthy, the upper class, who were much like the Buckinghams themselves. Lakshmi didn't fear being recognized. None of these snotty Englishmen would have thought it possible that such a lowly woman like Lakshmi would travel on the same ship with them. And for those that glanced at her several times, perhaps wondering in their respective minds what the dusky woman was doing among such distinguished company, none was bold enough to strike up a conversation with her.

Lakshmi was glad for that. She would use the long duration of the journey to examine herself and make sure her return to Kerala was a new page in the story that was her life.

It didn't take her long to find her cabin below deck. It was a small room furnished luxuriously to be comfortable for the well-paying passenger. Lakshmi sat on the bed just as the foghorn sounded again, alerting the passengers yet to board that the journey was about to begin. She wondered if she should join the passengers above, those waving goodbye to their loved ones on the docks.

It was almost midday when the ship began to sail, blasting its foghorn again as it moved almost imperceptibly away from the port. Lakshmi felt the ship's movement underneath

CHAPTER 8   222

her feet, and she reached out a hand to steady herself. Sitting on the chair by the bed, she couldn't help but wonder if she was the only passenger who had chosen to remain in their cabin.

If Lakshmi's memory served her correctly, the journey from India to England had taken quite a while. And the ship had docked in several places, stopping to take on supplies and passengers sometimes. The memories from that trip came to Lakshmi unbidden the more she spent aboard the ship. She found herself searching the faces of the crew, looking to see if she could recognize any of them from her previous trip, even if the chances were slim. She remembered the avuncular captain, a cheerful man called Mordecai Fletcher. And she remembered the advice he had given her that night when Lord Michael had had one of his infamous fits with the crew. Lakshmi smiled grimly and shook her head. Time was an illusion. You blinked, and the world changed

CHAPTER 8   223

before your very eyes.

This was a different ship and a different crew. They were much more formal, giving polite smiles and nods and only speaking when told. They were nothing like the Jezebel crew, the cheery and rambunctious bunch who had sung and jested along with the passengers, their voices ringing far out over the water, bringing joy and happiness to all aboard the ship.

The memories from that time were bittersweet. She had loved being on the ship, travelling and marvelling at the way the vessel cut through the water like a sword, at the sound of the waves crashing against themselves and the hull of the ship, and at the pleasant camaraderie of the company aboard, even though her awe had been tinged with darkness in the person of Lord Michael.

During the trip, his black temper had surfaced more times than Lakshmi could count, singling him out among the passengers as a problematic individual. The crew and the captain much

CHAPTER 8   224

disliked him. To him, they were a lousy lot. Smelly sailors below him were not supposed to be around companies like his. He had berated Lakshmi several times when she had sung with them or paused to speak with one of them or exchange a polite word. Lord Michael had been proud, too proud for one who was drowning in debt and was on the verge of disgrace. He barked at anyone he suspected was beneath him in class and sneered at those who disagreed with his views. Lakshmi had been ashamed that she was attached to him, doing everything she could at that time to prevent an already embarrassing scene from progressing into an uncontrollable situation. She had failed to do so that one time with Yóukè when they had come to blows on the deck in front of the crew.

Thinking about Yòuké did something to Lakshmi. It gave her a reaction that was at once familiar and foreign. It shocked her that she felt that way about someone she hadn't seen. It was the same feeling she had when they met on the

Jezebel, Yòuké running into her accidentally, knocking the dishes in her hands to the floor, and then helping her pick them up even while his mesmerizing brown eyes held hers spellbound. She had been so tongue-tied that she had struggled to string words together. And then he had been nothing but a gentleman the entire time he'd travelled with them. And Lord Michael had hated the man with a fierce intensity.

Looking back, Lakshmi imagined how she must have seemed in his eyes and the eyes of the crew as she stood by Lord Michael, even while it was clear he was in the wrong. They hadn't understood then that she had a duty in England. Lady Michelle had needed her help. And so she had refused the intriguing man's advances and urged him to follow him so they could begin their lives afresh. Lakshmi remembered the hurt she had seen in Yòuké's eyes the night she had declined his request. If only she had known her future in the

CHAPTER 8 226

Buckingham manor, she would have abandoned Lord Michael and gotten off the ship with Yòuké when they stopped momentarily at Cape Agulhas.

She had watched him leave the ship, misty-eyed and deeply saddened when she realized that she might never see him again. Then Lord Michael had come upon her like a foul smell, almost physically dragging her away from where she stood watching Yòuké's receding form. Her role as a caregiver had been too important to give up, a regretful decision if there ever was one.

Lakshmi left her cabin below deck and made her way up, her mind still weighed down by memories of the early days when she had seen the first signs of the darkness that would ultimately overshadow her. She climbed the stairs absently, faintly hearing the chatter of conversation she thought was coming through the walls or above deck.

The sun was high in the sky, but a cool breeze

CHAPTER 8 227

blew across the deck, causing the sails to undulate gently. Others were above deck, men and women enjoying themselves in the pleasant heat. And laughter drifted from several groups standing together, amusement evident in the chuckles that grated on Lakshmi's nerves. She moved towards the railings and away from the group, mildly berating herself for taking offence at their joviality. They were not the cause of her misfortune. Gloomy as she was, Lakshmi appreciated the beauty before her: the deep colour of the sea and the froth and the way the sun glinted off the waves as if they were made of sapphires.

Lakshmi sighed and closed her eyes, feeling the breeze blow through her hair and the salt spray caress her cheeks. Then she heard the sound of approaching footsteps, and her eyes flew open, and she whirled around and gasped in disbelief.

"Yòuké," she breathed, suddenly weak at the knees.

CHAPTER 8   228

"Surely this is a trick upon my eyes."

That voice. It was him. Yòuké. Lakshmi stumbled and reached out a hand towards the railing to steady herself. She shook off the vertigo and stared up at his face, speechless.

"But it is no trick. You're truly here," he said, a small smile on his face. "Hello, Lakshmi."

"Hello...Yòuké," she stuttered.

What strange magic was this? She had only thought about him a moment ago. And now here he was, in the flesh, smiling that charming smile that set her heart racing. Had she conjured him somehow? Lakshmi had been away from Kerala for a while, but she had not forgotten her grandmother's tales of magic, stories of spirits and beings that hung around one, sly and full of mischief, granting wishes and desires that often put the wisher in trouble.

But she hadn't wished to see Yòuké, had she?

"You don't seem too happy to see me," said Yòuké, failing to hide the hurt in his voice. "That's...something."

She was happy to see him, she realized all of a sudden. "I'm sorry, Yòuké. Of course, I am."

She moved closer to him to reinforce her words and entered his embrace as though it was the most natural thing in the world. Yòuké's strong arms around her felt fantastic. His masculine fragrance wrapped around her like a shawl, pleasant and comforting, and Lakshmi suddenly wanted to weep.

She held on for as long as was polite. And then she let him go reluctantly, blinking to stop the tears from spilling down her face.

"What are you doing here, Yòuké?" she asked, stretching her lips into a smile.

"I could ask you the same," replied Yòuké.

Lakshmi was aware that they had drawn an audience now. She didn't mind at all. They were the oddest couple on deck at that moment. They were dressed in the fashion of the upper-class English, in delicate garments and with courtly manners, but it was clear from their features that they were not English. And Yòuké looked so

CHAPTER 8   230

handsome, she had almost forgotten how good-looking he was. He had an aristocratic air, a high brow that told of his intelligence, and bright eyes that twinkled with amusement and humour but had the potential to become cold and piercing when his temper was roused.

Lakshmi looked away to hide the flush that had risen to her cheeks. There was no need to get flustered thinking about him.

"So, you are happy to see me," Yòuké said snugly.

"Ah, I can see your ego hasn't lessened one bit. Careful, you might fall off the ship if your head gets too big."

Yòuké chuckled, and Lakshmi was thrilled that she had made him laugh.

"No, it hasn't. But it is wonderful to see you."

"Likewise, Yòuké. And I mean it. When did you know it was me?"

"When you came on deck and scowled at the people laughing."

Lakshmi groaned. "I most certainly did not

scowl."

"Glared, then. You glared at them fiercely."

"I guess I did," Lakshmi conceded, grinning.

If he had seen that, he had seen her walk away, meaning he knew she was limping now. Her smile died slowly on her lips. Lakshmi didn't know how to think about that. She felt suddenly self-conscious, folding her hands protectively in front of her, an action that didn't go unnoticed by him. He reached for her gently, making Lakshmi's heart beat faster. He placed cool fingers on her arm and then carefully pulled her hands apart, opening her up to him and letting her know there was nothing to fear or hide from him. The warmth in his eyes eased her considerably, and Lakshmi returned his smile. He held on for a moment longer, and she savoured the feeling of his fingers on her skin.

The air between them thickened as though charged with the pull of attraction they both felt. Lakshmi realized suddenly that they had become the centre of attraction, then she cleared

CHAPTER 8   232

her throat and took a step back, wondering when the gap between both of them had reduced to about the length of an inch. Yòuké looked like he had just come out of a trance, blinking several times until his eyes sharpened again.

Lakshmi was glad she wasn't the only one affected by whatever was wrong with them. He took another step back, a movement that filled Lakshmi with a heady rush of feminine power.

They were quiet for a while, letting the silence between them bloom with the pleasant memories they had made on the Jezebel and the promise of their chance meeting. Lakshmi looked at him closely and as furtively as she could. Yòuké had changed. He was older, for sure. And he was more...present. He had all the time in the world as though he had accomplished all he had set out to do. And now he was going on with life, like a leaf floating atop a stream, subject to its ebb and flow. But there was a tightness to his eyes, and Lakshmi guessed he had seen his share of troubles. No

CHAPTER 8   233

one went through life unblooded.

"You've changed," he said after a while.

Lakshmi figured he was doing the same thing to her, trying to figure out what was going on in her mind and the things she had experienced that had scarred her. What would she tell him? And where could she start from?

"So have you," she replied. "You have some grey in your hair now." She was teasing him. His hair was as dark as she remembered, thick, curly and dark as sin.

He lifted his hand halfway, self-conscious all of a sudden. Then he saw the mischievous twinkle in her eyes and lowered his hand.

"Nicely done," he said. "I was wondering if you still had that sharp wit of yours. Glad to know it's present and maybe even sharper."

"Best be wary then," said Lakshmi, grinning. "I would not want to spill even one drop of that precious blue blood."

Yòuké tutted. "Come now, we have the same colour blood flowing through our veins. Red.

CHAPTER 8   234

And I'm not the only one dressed as though they have a footman standing around somewhere twiddling his thumbs and waiting for Madam to give him a task."

He made a show of looking around in search of said footman, and Lakshmi smacked him playfully on the arm." Please. You know what I mean. It does look like commerce has done you much good."

He gave a modest shrug. "It puts the garments on my back."

"Such fine garments, if I might add."

They continued in that manner, teasing and taunting one another pleasantly, and Lakshmi wondered how it was that she could still laugh so gaily even after all the darkness she had seen.

She had forgotten entirely that Yòuké was a creature of charm. It leaked from his pores like a fragrant perfume. She happily put her hands in his as they strolled on deck, mindful of the looks the others shot their way, especially the women folk who, it seemed, had never seen a man from the Orient as tall and solidly built as Yòuké. They were eating him up with their eyes. Lakshmi doubted if they saw her at all. And if they did, then there was undeniable envy in their gazes.

"I must exercise care on this ship," she said drily.

Yòuké turned around and stared at her, furrowing his brows. "Why do you say that?"

"Do you not see that you're being ogled, Yòuké?"

"Oh," he muttered, looking around. "I see. But why should you be careful?"

"A dinner knife in the back, for one. Or, I might trip up and accidently and fall off the railings or down the stairs." Lakshmi could see the shock and amusement in his eyes that she could speak about such things flippantly. But she didn't care. It was better he knew that she wasn't that naive village girl from Kerala he had met on the Jezebel anymore. Wait till he hears that I've been in prison, she thought darkly.

CHAPTER 8   236

Yòuké chuckled and shook his head. "I don't think you have to worry about that, Lakshmi."

"Oh, I do. You're not shocked by the attention." Lakshmi noted. "Not a new experience for you, I imagine."

"Well, the boldness of the English woman, especially those from the upper class, is no news. Let's say I'm no stranger to brazen advances and secret confrontations."

"How is it that you're not yet dead from a duel? Their husbands must be intimidated by you."

"On the contrary," Yòuké said quickly. "I've run from a few, Lakshmi. I do value my life. Besides, these snobby women do not impress me. They're pretty on the surface, but there's no depth to them."

"So, you're not married then?" Lakshmi ventured. "I did not see a ring." She had looked. Some men took off their bands all the time. Women too. But Yòuké wasn't the dishonourable sort. Still...

CHAPTER 8 237

"You checked," Yòuké grinned. "No, I'm not married."

"Shame," Lakshmi mumbled, turning away to hide her smile.

"You're not married either."

"What gave me away?"

"Well, no man is hovering around you, threatening to bludgeon me over the head. And you're not wearing a ring."

"Right." Lakshmi sighed. "Not married either."

"And why is that?"

She stared at him for a while, then she shrugged. Let him interpret that how he wants. But she was not telling him anything now, not yet. They had just become reacquainted. Yòuké didn't press for details, gratefully. Lakshmi didn't know if he saw the pain in her eyes and imagined she would not want to talk about it, but he stood by her silently and watched the waves with her.

"So, where are you heading to?" she asked.

"I have some interests I would like to check on

CHAPTER 8   238

in Africa," Yòuké said, leaning on the railings. "My associates talk of a place, the Gold Coast."

"Interesting," said Lakshmi.

There was a pause, in which a strange look came into Yòuké's eyes. "Do you...?" He hesitated.

"Yes?"

"Nothing, never mind."

Lakshmi wondered for a while what he had been about to say. Did she know about the Gold Coast? The answer was no. She hadn't travelled much. She hadn't been anywhere else but England and India. But that was nothing to be ashamed of.

He interrupted her, musing with a question. "And what about you?"

"What?"

"Where are you headed?" Yòuké asked softly.

There was only one answer. And emotion welled in her chest as she thought about it. She didn't know why she was suddenly overwhelmed by her feelings. It was probably

CHAPTER 8 239

because of the manner in which he had asked. Gently, as if he knew in some way all that had happened, she was going back to Kerala.

"Home," she whispered. "I'm going home."

During dinner that night, while seated across from each other at the large table around which most of the passengers dining with them sat conversing, Yòuké had eyes only for the woman in front of him. She ate sparingly, lifting the spoon to take measured bites at intervals. The conversation flowed around them as the other diners introduced themselves and their interests amid the sound of cutlery in China. Candles burned brightly on the table and walls, glinting off bracelets and jewellery around wrists and necks.

Several of the crew seemed to be adept musicians, which wasn't strange to Yòuké. Too much time spent at sea could drive a man mad. Things like drink and music kept that madness at bay. They played fantastically, setting a cheery mood as Yòuké and the others ate. But

CHAPTER 8 240

Lakshmi didn't seem too impressed, Yòuké noted. She would smile at a humorous comment made by one of the people dining with them, then the smile would pass quickly, and her eyes would take on a distant look, as though she wasn't entirely in the present or as though she was relieving a memory that wasn't too pleasant.

Yòuké wished he could talk to her, find out the reason for that haunting look that was beneath the cool mask she had put on since he'd seen her on deck. It had been such a pleasure to see her. Slightly taken aback by the sudden appearance of the woman he had had dreams about since he had first laid eyes on, he had thought how fortuitous it was to see her again, especially now in his life when he had reached such a point where he wanted to build a family of his own. And then he'd spoken to her and seen the spark of interest in her eyes to tell him she still found him attractive. But there were shadows there, too in her eyes. And the limp...

CHAPTER 8   241

He had thought deeply about how to broach the topic with her. And he had discarded all the ideas except one. He would ask her directly what she had been up to all this while and what happened in England. Yòuké remembered the unpleasant man Lakshmi had travelled with. He ground his teeth in annoyance when it occurred to him that Lord Michael could be blamed for whatever happened to Lakshmi.

Yòuké played with the rest of the food because his appetite had suddenly vanished thinking of the man. He dropped the spoon and leaned back in his chair, eyes fixed on Lakshmi. She must have known he was looking at her because she avoided his gaze and looked everywhere but in his direction. But he had to talk to her. He couldn't wait till they had some privacy to ask her the questions he had been nursing for a while.

"You're not eating, sir."

Yòuké's head whipped to the right at the sound of the lilting voice beside him. He was seated

CHAPTER 8   242

between two people, a taciturn man on his left and a beautiful woman with striking features on his right. Her dress was deliberately cut in a manner that bared her neck and the tops of her breasts. Yòuké was concerned that she would fall out of the dress if she leaned towards him too much. He did well to keep his eyes above her neck. He'd rather not have wine splashed in his face for a perceived wrong on the woman's honour, even though she was offering her...jewels so freely.

"Excuse me?" he mumbled.

"The food," she said, gesturing at his plate. "It's not to your liking?"

"Oh, it's fantastic," Yòuké said. "The cook outdid himself. Or herself," amended Yòuké after a while. "You're not the cook, are you?"

"No," said the woman, chuckling lightly. "But I agree with you. Why are you not eating then?"

What could he tell her? He was worried about Lakshmi and wondered about her past and what she had been through.

CHAPTER 8 243

"Just deep in thought, is all. Thanks."

"I see," she said, even if she clearly didn't see.

Yòuké turned away pointedly, a sign that he didn't want to converse with anyone. Anyone that wasn't Lakshmi, that was.

"So, where are you from?" questioned the woman.

Yòuké answered politely and asked his question, all the while mindful of Lakshmi's presence on the other side of the table. And then, the food was cleared away, and the tempo of the music increased. Several people got up, hands reaching out to their partners, and both parties stepped forward to dance. Yòuké knew the lady beside him—whose name he had already forgotten—was waiting for him to ask her to dance. And he was reluctant to do so. But then he saw from the corner of his eyes as a handsome, well-dressed man approached Lakshmi, whispered politely to her and insisted on dancing. Lakshmi stood up and went with him, and Yòuké battled to concentrate even as

CHAPTER 8 244

the lady beside him chatted about something.

He couldn't stand it any longer. "Would you like to dance?"

"Oh, yes!"

Yòuké stood up in a flash and held out a hand. He led the woman towards the area where the music was loud, and the others were dancing. He saw Lakshmi immediately with the man's hands around her, and it felt like a blow to his stomach when he saw the bright smile on her face. Struggling to suppress the piercing stab of jealousy, he pasted a smile on his face and led the woman in a dance. She pressed herself up on him and grabbed his arms so tightly that Yòuké winced. He tried not to look down on her too much. He could see everything.

Then the tempo switched to a slower one, and they had to exchange partners. Yòuké made a beeline for Lakshmi and her partner, and the switch happened so smoothly that it didn't even look as if Yòuké orchestrated it. Then Lakshmi was in his arms, and it felt...wonderful.

CHAPTER 8   245

He gave a light squeeze and they both chuckled when she gave him one in return.

*****

"Your friend doesn't look too happy," Lakshmi whispered. "She's glaring daggers at us."

"I can't say I care," Yòuké said cheerily.

He honestly didn't care, Lakshmi noted. She had watched the woman virtually drape herself on him all night as though she was a shawl, utterly oblivious to Yòuké's discomfort all the while, even if it was evident to everybody else.

"You almost fell down her bodice," said Lakshmi. "Like Alice in Wonderland."

"Thankfully, I didn't," said Yòuké. "There's no wonder there for sure. Look at it. It's a death trap."

She pinched him on the arm, and Yòuké's quiet laughter somehow rumbled in his chest and hers, tickling her to her toes.

"I only have eyes for one woman tonight," he said much more seriously, leaning back to stare

CHAPTER 8 246

intently into her eyes. "And she's not the one."

"Oh, Yòuké," Lakshmi whispered, looking away. "Don't say things like that."

"Why?"

She remained silent. How could she tell him that she had just come out of a harrowing ordeal and still bore the scars to show it? Could he deal with the baggage she carried? And above all, was she ready to commit to something with him even now that her future was uncertain?

These questions weighed heavily on her as they swayed together in time with the music and the ship. Then Yòuké leaned back and whispered to her.

"How about we go somewhere else? I can tell you're tired. Maybe some air would do you some good."

And she was exhausted. She had not entirely healed from her injuries, especially the one on her thigh. She let Yòuké lead her out of the dining room and towards the upper deck. They stepped out into the cool night, and Lakshmi was glad to be away from the heat and noise. She breathed the cold air in, letting it sit in her lungs for a while. She closed her eyes and savoured the feeling.

She didn't realize she was leaning forward until she felt Yòuké strong hands on her arm, holding her back from falling on her face.

"Careful," Yòuké said kindly.

"I'm sorry," she whispered.

"Don't apologize. Maybe dancing on with a leg injury wasn't such a great idea. Here, this is better."

Yòuké approached her and gently pulled her back until she leaned into him. Lakshmi sighed in appreciation as his arms came around her, and he held her carefully. They stood that way for a while. Lakshmi was grateful for the strength in Yòuké's arms and the quiet assurance he offered. She could imagine the cogs in his head turning, going over the questions he wanted to ask. Yòuké was a considerate man, sensible and very observant.

CHAPTER 8   248

She didn't think his opinion of her would change if she told him about her ordeal. But she was also wary.

She had once misjudged a man's character, someone she had thought she knew utterly. The thought of making the same mistake with Yòuké was too painful to imagine. She couldn't bear it if he looked at her with questions in his eyes. Being accused of murder was no small thing. And Yòuké had not been there. Why would he believe her if she stated her innocence to him?

"You're tense."

She had forgotten that she was leaning into his solid chest. She forced herself to relax and not overthink. If he asked her, she was going to tell him. But if he didn't, then...

"What happened, Lakshmi?" Yòuké asked gently. "Why did you leave England and Lord Michael's household?"

There it was, the moment she had dreaded since she'd laid eyes on Yòuké again. Where would she start from?

CHAPTER 8 249

"If you're uncomfortable talking about it—"

"No," Lakshmi said softly. "It's just that... it's too painful to recall." Her voice was barely a whisper, but Yòuké still heard her.

"Then you don't have to say anything if it will cause you much pain. I'm sorry I asked."

"Don't be, Yòuké. I'll tell you. It's in the past, after all." She said, even though it had barely been a week.

She gathered her wits about her, grateful when Yòuké tightened his hold on her. She drew strength from his action and began right from when Yòuké had left the ship at the cape. In the middle of her tragic tale, when she felt him freeze, she left the comfort of his arms and continued to speak. She had to pause at certain places to catch her breath and stop the tears from dripping down her cheeks.

There were others on deck now, couples wanting a breath of fresh air before bed. But Lakshmi and Yòuké had as much privacy as they could get.

CHAPTER 8   250

When she thought she had her emotions under control, she continued with the story, telling her quiet but attentive listener how she had been locked up with the most vile women and how she'd been beaten up several times until she had had to stand up for herself at some point. She told him all about Geoffrey and Todd, about every single thing that had happened between her and the both of them.

"...then Lord Michael told me one night at the manor that I was free to go. He...compensated me for all that I had gone through. And I left the manor and bought a ticket to India shortly after that."

The sounds of the waves crashing against the hull and the lull of quiet conversation were the only sounds that reached Lakshmi's ears as she watched the undulating water. She could feel Yòuké's presence behind her. And she could tell that he was angry. But what or who was he angry at?

She didn't dare turn around to look at him. She

wouldn't be able to bear it if his anger was directed at her. Maybe he felt some way about Todd or even Geoffrey. But he had been nowhere in the picture when she had been with Todd. She hadn't even thought she would ever lay eyes on his person again.

"Lakshmi," his voice was hoarse behind her.

"Please, look at me."

She hesitated for a second, then turned slowly, her head still lowered. She felt the air stir as he walked up to her. Then she felt his warm fingers under her chin, and he lifted her face to stare into her eyes. She almost cried when she saw the sympathy and the pain he felt for her in his eyes. He wasn't angry at her. Not at all.

"I'm not a violent man by any chance," he whispered hoarsely, his minty breath caressing her face. "But I do feel a strong urge to do great harm to the Buckinghams when I get my hands on them."

Lakshmi smiled sadly. "It's all in the past, Yòuké."

CHAPTER 8   252

"I know. But they hurt you so much. They deserve much more than has happened to them."

"Yes, they do."

"I'm so sorry, my darling," Yòuké whispered, pulling her into a fierce hug. "For everything."

Then, Lakshmi let the tears flow, hot tears that fell from her eyes and soaked into Yòuké's shirt. His warm palms traced delicious patterns on her back, soothing her until the pain lessened and she was warm on the inside. Eyes closed and still nestled in Yòuké's arms, she smiled when she realized how relieved she was that nothing was hidden from him. She had trusted her gut that he would be on her side. She held him tighter and was ecstatic when he tightened his hold on her.

They swayed with the ship, quiet and deeply aware of each other. Then Lakshmi stifled a yawn, and Yòuké chuckled.

"I think the lady is sleepy," Yòuké drawled.

"She is," Lakshmi said, grinning into Yòuké's shirt. "I'm a tad overwhelmed, Yòuké. You

CHAPTER 8   253

might have to carry me to my cabin."

"Gladly," Yòuké whispered, reaching down to lift her gently.

"I'm kidding!" Lakshmi squealed, laughing and pushing his hands away. "I can very well walk on my own, Yòuké."

"Fine," Yòuké said, offering his arm for support.

Yòuké walked her below deck and to her door and politely stepped back when Lakshmi placed her hand on the knob.

She turned around shyly and gazed up at him. Then she took a bold step forward and went on tiptoes to kiss his cheek. Then she stood back and said, "Thank you, sir. For...tonight."

"You're welcome, Lakshmi. Good night, my lady."

He bowed and waited for her to step into her cabin and shut the door, then he turned around and walked away with a broad smile.

Lakshmi woke up feeling better than she had felt since she had been on the ship. She tossed

CHAPTER 8 254

aside the covers and stretched like a cat. Then she caught herself and realized that she was smiling. She shook her head and collapsed onto her bed, mindful of how light she was inside. She knew she was feeling this way because of Yòuké. It was a refreshing feeling to have him comfort her. She had loved being in his arms, and for the first time in a long time, she felt a tad optimistic about her future, even though she couldn't say if Yòuké would be in it. And she realized then that she wanted him to be in it.

Lakshmi was aware of the blossoming feeling between the both of them. And it was different this time around. There was no one to ruin what they had or to get in the way. Nothing. Except her past, maybe. That was one dark thought she couldn't help but entertain. Still, she struggled internally with the thought. Why must she let her past dictate her future? Yòuké had been a gentleman the whole time, understanding and comforting her when she was most vulnerable.

A knock on her door pulled her out of her

thoughts. It didn't feel like the ship was in motion, and Lakshmi could hear the din of raised voices and loud laughter. It sounded to her like a marketplace was on the other side of the boat. They had docked somewhere. She stood up and got her robe, putting it on warily and walking to her door. The knock sounded again, and she waited a second before opening the door slightly.

It was a crew member, a boy on the cusp of adulthood. He flushed when Lakshmi blinked at him.

"Yes?"

"Morning, m'lady. I was told to inform you that you will be going on a boat cruise this morning and that the lady should kindly dress appropriately."

"A cruise? Off the ship?"

"Yes, ma'am."

"Me? That's a tad strange. Who told you to inform me?" Lakshmi asked warily, narrowing her eyes.

CHAPTER 8   256

The boy gulped and said, "The gentleman, ma'am."

"The gentleman," Lakshmi parroted.

It was unusual that a merchant ship would dock and let its passengers go on a boat cruise. They were usually on a schedule, seeing as how passengers had places to be and cargo on board that had to be delivered by a set time.

"How odd," Lakshmi said aloud and to herself.

Then she realized the boy was waiting for her, and she thanked him and sent him on his way.

She shut the door and sat on her bed, knowing this gentleman was Yòuké. She couldn't help but feel as though the cruise was for her benefit, no matter how narcissistic that sounded to her ears. The boy had said to dress appropriately. Lakshmi made her box and hefted it onto her bed. She searched for a garment suitable for a boat cruise. She finally settled on something she thought would do, and then she added gloves that reached up to her elbows to the ensemble. It was flattering enough not to make her look drab,

CHAPTER 8 257

but it covered up enough of her to protect against mosquitos and insect bites if they were where she thought they were. She drove to close her box when she saw a rolled-up piece of paper among her clothes. She picked it up and sat beside her open box, unrolling it.

She knew what it was. A note Todd had left for her the morning after they had spent time together in the orchard. Lakshmi couldn't help but feel embarrassed as she reread the note. To think that she had done such a thing with him was shocking to her now. She liked to think it was inevitable, especially with how both of them had been, facing challenges together and managing to overcome them. The orchard had been a celebration, a memory to cherish and finally, a way to say farewell. She hadn't thought about that time in the orchard since that first day on the ship. She had been distracted by Yòuké and swept away by his charm. She had only thought about Todd in passing and not in the manner she was doing now.

CHAPTER 8   258

She tossed the letter on the small table beside her bed, suddenly feeling as though she was being unfaithful to Yòuké by simply thinking about Todd. She reminded herself immediately that she was not Yòuké's wife or his mistress, and the thing with Todd was in the past. It wouldn't make much sense for her to dwell on it or even think about it.

She closed her eyes and sighed, forcing all thoughts of Todd aside. It wasn't difficult to do, seeing as she was very attracted to Yòuké. And she was going on a boat cruise with him. Her excitement came as a shock to her. It was such a foreign thing to feel after all the bad things that had happened to her. She felt like a child again, looking forward to the sweet cakes her grandmother used to give her when she came to visit.

A pang of longing tugged at her heart. She couldn't wait to be back in Kerala, where the language was like music to her eyes, and the faces were like her own. She missed it so much

CHAPTER 8 259

and wondered momentarily if time had changed it just as it had changed her. She had left as a girl, and she was now a woman. Things would not be the same. And that saddened her a little. But that was the way life worked. Change was inevitable. That was as certain as the sun rising in the east and setting in the west.

But Lakshmi was prepared to brave it out. This budding thing with Yòuké first, then whatever came next.

*****

They were in Africa. Lakshmi had never been on the continent but she had heard so many interesting tales about it. She came off the ship with Yòuké, who was so happy he grinned from ear to ear, hailing the locals who worked on the docks and the cargo men who called out various versions of his name Lakshmi had never heard of. They were all very respectful and it was evident he was well loved and was no stranger to the place. Yòuké basked in the attention, waving and speaking the language to some of

CHAPTER 8   260

the men.

"It's like you're at home here," Lakshmi murmured when they walked past.

Yòuké shrugged. "You would not be wrong in saying so. This is my home. All the ports on our route are."

"And the language? I had no idea I was with a polyglot."

"Well, prepare to be shocked, my lady. You're in for a treat."

There seemed to be a spring to his steps, and his excitement was infectious. When he had come for Lakshmi earlier, and she had opened the door as soon as he knocked, she eyed him appreciatively, wondering how he had managed to look so gentlemanly and rugged at the same time. Then he'd taken her hands and led her from her cabin to the upper deck to show her the paradise they had entered.

Africa was beautiful, and the air was unspoiled and redolent with exotic smells.

The water was a healthy aquamarine, and the

CHAPTER 8 261

verdant trees and forests that stretched as far as the eyes could see was a sight Lakshmi would never forget. The view was breathtaking. Then Yòuké had come up beside her to whisper in her ear that she had not seen all of it yet.

Now, they were heading into the market close to the docks and would get on the cruise boat at the other end of the market, much closer to the forests. Lakshmi was enthralled.

The market was a lively hub of activity, and Lakshmi and Yòuké weren't the only foreign couple present. The colourful wares on display thrilled Lakshmi's eyes: bales of clothing heaped as tall as a tower, all of it in a myriad of colours Lakshmi hadn't seen until that moment, exotic fruits that looked so strange Lakshmi was a tad hesitant to touch them. The people were jovial and welcoming, their ebony skins glinting under the brilliant sun and their smiles broadening when Yòuké spoke to them in their language.

Lakshmi took all of the sights in like a starving

CHAPTER 8   262

woman. It was not very different from the market in Kerala. Yòuké produced a fruit from out of nowhere and offered her a bite, his eyes alight with mischief, prodding her gently when she protested. Then she gave in and took a bite, and her taste buds exploded into a thousand pieces. Even as Yòuké laughed heartily at the expression of wonder and awe on her face, Lakshmi thought she had never tasted anything so fantastic.

Then they got to the market's spice section, and Lakshmi almost cried at the rush of memories the smells evoked. If she had closed her eyes and inhaled, she could have imagined that she was in Kerala in front of her grandmother's kiosk. Yòuké must have understood her feelings, and he gave her a moment to gather herself, only moving when she was ready to go.

They were on the boat instantly, a small, sturdy vessel that was low in the water and manned by an elderly man with a mischievous smile. He wore a wide-brimmed raffia hat. And he gave

Lakshmi and Yòuké hats of their own to keep off the sun, which could get a bit hot.

They set off from shore, keeping close to the giant trees and the shade they offered. Yòuké briefly discussed with the man, laughing gaily with him while Lakshmi looked at everything with wonder in her eyes. The forest itself was alive, it seemed. The sounds of wildlife reverberated and reached her ears, managing to frighten and thrill her simultaneously. She thought could see shapes in the trees, monkeys and other small animals that called the rich forest home.

Then she realized that the conversation had ceased, and the man had moved to the rear of the boat, offering Lakshmi and Yòuké some privacy. The ship moved so smoothly on the water and so silently, too. The branches of the enormous trees reflected off the water's surface, and Lakshmi couldn't help but suppress a shiver at the sheer delight she was experiencing.

She settled into Yòuké's arms as they glided

through the forest, and then the man began to hum a quiet tune that merged so smoothly with the sounds emanating from the forest. Lakshmi hated interrupting the mood, but she could no longer keep her curiosity at bay.

"What's he saying?" she asked.

She felt Yòuké tilt his head, and then he said a moment later, "He's singing to the forest gods. He's asking them for a favour. Several."

"Oh?"

"Yes, good crops this season, a barn full of...grain, I think. And children." Yòuké chuckled. "He's asking for children but not for himself."

It took a while for Lakshmi to grasp the implication of Yòuké's statement. What a mischievous man their guide was.

"Do you want children, Lakshmi?" Yòuké asked softly.

"Yes," she said, "Someday."

Yòuké was too silent, which told Lakshmi that he wanted to say something important, which made her nervous for some reason.

"So, do you bring all your conquests here, sir?" she asked to fill the silence.

"W-what?" Yòuké sputtered.

Lakshmi chuckled and repeated herself.

"Of course," Yòuké said with a smile in his voice. "There's something in the water that just does the magic. Or maybe it's the trees. I don't know."

Lakshmi giggled and shook her head.

"No one," he said more seriously. "I've brought no one here. I usually come on my own."

"That's rather sad," Lakshmi said.

"Is it?"

"Yes. It's an experience that would be more enjoyable if shared with someone else."

"I always have the guide with me," Yòuké jested. "He's a great company."

Lakshmi sighed and rolled her eyes. "You know what I mean, Yòuké. Female company. A lady."

CHAPTER 8   266

His smile was cheeky. "Oh, I didn't realize that was what you meant."

"Right." Lakshmi grinned. "So, why?"

Yòuké was silent for a while, and Lakshmi had thought he wouldn't answer until he said, "It just didn't happen. Business was my primary focus, and..."

"And?"

"Let's say I still nursed my feelings for a certain woman."

"And who would that be?" she asked, even if she knew the answer.

"You, Lakshmi."

"Oh," was all Lakshmi said. She didn't know how to respond. But she was incredibly flattered.

She heard and felt Yòuké's deep laughter and snuggled closer to him. "Tell me about your trips, Yòuké. All of them."

"Hmm, let's see."

She listened to his voice as he told one story after another. He said the ones that had her quaking with laughter, causing their guide to turn around and give them a questioning look. And he told the one that had her crying, even though it had a beautiful and touching ending. Yòuké had been all over the world, it seemed. And he had managed to stay safe while doing so.

"Hold on, darling," he said a moment later.

Lakshmi was reluctant to leave his embrace, but she did so and turned around to see what he was doing. He reached for a basket Lakshmi hadn't even noticed and pulled it closer to them. He removed the lid and presented the basket to Lakshmi. It was a basket of fruits, cakes and sweets.

"Sustenance," he said triumphantly, eliciting a giggle from Lakshmi. She realized she was giggling a lot lately. Yòuké was humorous in his actions, and his wit was undeniably attractive.

He laid out a clean napkin and laid out one large plate in front of them. Then, he cut her fruit for her and fed her with a fork. He resumed

CHAPTER 8   268

his stories and paused at intervals to point out this animal, tree, fish, or bird. Lakshmi didn't realize so much time had passed until she saw that the sun had already passed its highest point in the sky and was heading towards the horizon.

The boat came ashore on another corner of the market, and the guide bid them farewell shortly after, whispering something to Yòuké that had both men laughing raucously.

"What did he say?"

Yòuké chuckled in remembrance and said, "He said the gods would give us children with strong legs."

"What?"

Yòuké shrugged, "That's a real thing here. Strong-legged kids and everything would be all right."

Lakshmi laughed and entwined her arm in his. They walked through the market slowly this time around. They were pausing to admire the wares closely. Yòuké bought her an ivory bangle and a necklace to follow. And Lakshmi

CHAPTER 8 269

bought him a handmade knife made from a stone in return. It was almost nightfall, and music was playing somewhere. It was the sound of drumbeats and raised voices that the wind carried to their hearing.

"What is that?" Lakshmi asked.

"Let's go see."

Yòuké led her towards the sound, weaving through the marketplace maze until they came close to the shore, where a bunch of locals gathered around a bonfire. People stood around clapping and singing along while women dressed in white garments and with white marks on their dark skins danced around the fire, their sonorous voices merging and touching something in Lakshmi's heart. The sound of the waves in the background and the cool breeze from the sea painted a haunting picture, along with the small crowd gathered.

"What are they saying?" Lakshmi asked.

Yòuké's brow furrowed in concentration. "It's in a dialect I'm not very familiar with. Give me a second."

They listened momentarily, and then Yòuké mumbled, "That's fascinating."

"What is?"

"The song. It's a song about new beginnings."

A chill travelled down Lakshmi's spine at that. What were the odds that she happened to be right there with Yòuké as the women sang?

"Truly, Yòuké?"

"Yes, Lakshmi. Positive."

Was this a sign for both of them? A cosmic signal, perhaps, that they should forget all that had happened and begin on a fresh slate. Lakshmi wanted so much to think that that was the case. She deserved a spell of happiness for a change, and they both did.

"That's truly fascinating," she said when she had recovered her voice. She stared up at him fondly and imagined that she could read his mind tonight, on this one special night that fate seemed to be working in tandem with the universe, pulling the both of them together right there on the shores of a beach in Africa.

She took Yòuké's hand in hers as they turned around and walked away from the crowd, turning their backs to the heat and the pleasant music, feeling the vibrations fade away until all they could hear was the wind and the waves. She wrapped the shawl around herself to keep the chill off, and Yòuké tutted and offered her his coat, which was thick and perfect.

"You're going to catch your death, sir," Lakshmi said, even while she eyed the coat and imagined herself wrapped in its delicious warmth. "I'll not be responsible for that."

Yòuké sighed and draped it over her shoulder, regardless of her protests. "You forget something important, dear lady."

"And what is that?"

"I'm a native, remember? Do not let my fine garments and flowery speech fool you. I'm a wild man."

Yòuké turned to look at her and gave her a smoulder, and Lakshmi broke into loud laughter

CHAPTER 8   272

that echoed and carried across the water. She paused to catch her breath, and Yòuké laughed beside her until they both lay on the cool sand and stared at the stars twinkling above the night sky. Their fingers were entwined, and the invisible bonds between them tightened around their hearts and dug deep, pulling them closer together.

"I used to do this when I was younger," said Lakshmi. "Very young. My grandmother would point at the stars and tell me stories about them. And it's interesting to think they're the same stars here, too. But I guess the stories would be different here."

"I guess so, too," reasoned Yòuké. "I can tell you a story about the stars, which would differ from the one you've heard. I guess what they have in common is that they're stories. And they mean something to each of us in our way."

"Absolutely," said Lakshmi. Yòuké couldn't be more accurate. She wondered what story the stars were telling them now. She sighed, satisfied and said, "I don't want the night to end."

Yòuké chuckled. "Me too. But I fear we must return before the captain sends a search party for us. And probably request more money for shaving off several years of his life..."

Lakshmi's ear twitched. "How long are we here for, Yòuké?"

"Here?"

"Yes, how long until we resume the journey?"

Yòuké shrugged and assumed an innocent expression. "That depends on the captain and his business."

"I heard you, you know. You didn't have to."

Yòuké sighed. "Come on, it was no trouble at all, Lakshmi. It's no skin off my nose." He stood up and dusted the sand off his trousers.

"Come on now, it's getting late." He offered a hand to Lakshmi and pulled her up gently; then, they walked hand in hand to where the ship had docked.

"You're not hungry, are you?" asked Yòuké, "I

CHAPTER 8   274

can get the cook to arrange something light for you."

"Heavens, no. I'm satisfied, Yòuké. If I eat anymore, I'm afraid the captain would mistake me for a barrel and roll me down to the cargo hold."

They stifled their chuckles and came aboard, quickly taking the quickest route to Lakshmi's cabin.

Lakshmi had had such a wonderful time, and the choice was hers how the night ended. But Yòuké was not pushy, and she loved him for it. He'd stopped the journey to take her on a boat cruise, and he had bought her gifts, fed her and entertained her with his stories and jokes. And now she was most certainly falling in love with him.

They got to the door of her cabin and turned around to stare into each other's eyes. Lakshmi had a request on her tongue, but she did not say it. She felt it was too soon.

Then Yòuké said in the dim quietness of the

hallway, "Lakshmi, please permit me to come to India with you."

CHAPTER 8

Long after Yòuké had gone to his cabin, Lakshmi lay awake in her bed under the covers. It was never hushed on the ship, and Lakshmi could hear the sailors singing drunkenly and laughing with the locals who had come on board for the night.

She had expected to fall asleep as soon as she climbed into bed. But then, she had gone over the conversation with Yòuké throughout the day and the question he had asked her just before he left. Lakshmi had not given him an answer, even if she knew what she wanted the most. She had hesitated for too long, and Yòuké had smiled sadly and apologized for being too forward. Then he'd bowed and walked away, leaving Lakshmi feeling like a heel.

In truth, she wanted him to come with her, or she wanted to go with him. Whichever. She wanted to be with Yòuké, and that was certain. But she didn't know why she had not said so when he'd asked. Something had prevented her but she didn't know what it was. That was why she was so uneasy, tossing and turning in bed, struggling to find a cool spot to settle into. She thought for a moment about leaving her room and going above deck. But she was too tired. And if she stepped out of her cabin, she knew she was heading straight to Yòuké's.

She sighed and threw off the covers, suddenly annoyed at herself. She stood up and began to pace, turning around almost in a circle. She sat down after a while and came to a resolution. She was going to tell Yòuké her mind tomorrow morning. Yes. She would love for him to come to India with her. She would go anywhere with him. She loved him.

This was the fresh start she needed. The woman's song on the beach made much more sense now, even if she didn't know the words. Yòuké had explained them to her. The universe was in support of them getting together. The realization filled Lakshmi with a substantial

CHAPTER 8   278

certainty. The thoughts that were running riot in her head stilled with that realization. She climbed into bed and laid her head on the pillow, praying for sleep to take her now that she'd stopped fretting over the plan of action. She closed her eyes and imagined she was still on that boat with Yòuké, sitting silently in his arms as the guide sang his songs and the boat glided over the water.

She had a brief flash of his face, handsome and welcoming. It was a face she had come to love so dearly.

Lakshmi smiled and snuggled deeper into her sheets. And then she saw the faces of her family in India. Rajan, her father, her mother Lata, and her sister Meena, who had been barely a teenager when Lakshmi had left Kerala. And she saw her uncle, aunts, and nieces and nephews smiling at her and telling her that they were waiting for her. Tears streamed down Lakshmi's cheeks even as her eyes were closed. Yòuké would be happy to see them. And they would love him as much as she had come to love him. Lakshmi's exhaustion overcame her, and she fell into a deep sleep.

The following morning, well-rested and refreshed, Lakshmi ate with the other passengers in the dining room. She had a healthy appetite, and she thought it was because of the pleasant African air. It took her only a second to realize that Yòuké wasn't dining with them. That concerned her, but she chose not to dwell on it for long. Lakshmi had heard from one of the crew mates that they would be docked for a few days, which was unusual but not unheard of. Then she remembered that Yòuké had said that his stop was somewhere in Africa, and she panicked for a second, wondering if her indecision yesterday had anything to do with his absence. If that wasn't the case, then where was he? It was very early morning, and Yòuké wasn't a heavy sleeper.

After breakfast, she went above deck and searched for Yòuké on the ship as furtively as she could. She couldn't find him. Then she searched for the young boy that Yòuké had sent to her. She found him hanging off a rope, and she drew his attention. He came swiftly to her and stood almost at attention.

"Have you seen Mr. Yòuké?" she asked politely.

"The gentleman?"

Lakshmi assumed he wasn't known as Yòuké around these parts. She was sure that sailors had a name for him, just like she had heard the locals call him the previous day.

"Yes, him."

"Oh, he left early, just before sunrise."

She didn't think it was proper to start questioning the poor boy about Yòuké's whereabouts like he was his wife. Yòuké was a grown man and could do what he wanted without her trailing after him like a lost puppy. Still, it wouldn't have hurt for him to leave her a message or note that he was going someplace.

She looked at the boy and asked, "He didn't

happen to leave a message for me, did he?"

The boy shook his head. "Not to me, ma'am."

Lakshmi nodded her thanks and turned away, suddenly worried about where he was and what was going through his mind in that very second. She wasn't going to go chasing after him. She checked for the voluptuous woman who had been eyeing Yòuké like a piece of meat she would love to bite into. Lakshmi hadn't thought to search for her at the table where she had had breakfast.

She found the woman somewhere else on the ship with her claws wrapped around another man, the one who had asked Lakshmi for a dance that evening. They were leaving the boat and heading into town, arm in arm. Lakshmi heaved a sigh of relief and wondered when she had become so possessive about Yòuké. She also asked if she would get lost if she left the ship. A part of her argued that she wasn't going in search of Yòuké; another part insisted that that was what she was doing and had every right

CHAPTER 8   282

to do so. It took her a while to decide, which was no decision.

But she didn't have to worry too much about what to do because Yòuké came bounding up the ramp an hour later, his dark hair ruffled and a broad smile. She saw him coming from afar and watched his expression as he searched for something.

Or someone, Lakshmi thought fondly. He was looking for her, and she would have missed him if she'd gone off the ship. His eyes found hers a moment later, and he approached her with a mischievous grin. Lakshmi took in his muddy apparel and wondered what he had been up to. He was dressed like one of the shop hands. He wore work boots and plain garments but was the most handsome man she had ever seen.

He stood in front of her and bowed slightly. "Good morning, Lakshmi. You look fantastic. Might I ask where you're headed and who you're going with?"

Lakshmi giggled and waved her hand. "Oh, no

one. And who might you be, mister?" she asked with mock seriousness. "I don't recall ever making your acquaintance."

"Only a lowly servant, madam," Yòuké said, mischief glinting in his eyes. "I could not bear to stay away any longer."

Lakshmi laughed and shook her head, "Stop, Yòuké. You're drawing a crowd."

"Let them look," he said, a measure of seriousness creeping into his voice.

"I was worried about you," Lakshmi said. "I wondered where you were."

Yòuké came closer, and she was hit with the heady mix of his scent, mud, leather and a pleasant fragrance she couldn't place.

"I had some business to attend to," said Yòuké apologetically. "I should have left a message for you so you wouldn't worry so much."

"I figured that that was the case," Lakshmi said.

A pause.

"Yòuké, yesterday..."

CHAPTER 8   284

"Hold on, Lakshmi," Yòuké said softly. "There's something I need to say."

He took her hands in his and held onto her lightly. "I shouldn't have asked that of you yesterday so soon after your experiences. It was selfish and insensitive of me, Lakshmi."

"Oh, Yòuké." An apology was the last thing she had expected from him, and to hear him speak so earnestly broke her heart into several pieces. "I'm the one who's meant to apologize. I should have answered you yesterday, but I was scared."

"Scared of what, darling?"

"I was uncertain, but I no longer am, Yòuké. My answer is yes. I want to be with you. In India or Africa."

She watched his blank features for a while, and then his lips stretched into a broad smile, and his eyes lit up from within with a fierce joy that shook Lakshmi to her core. He pulled her into his arms and kissed her on the mouth until she thought she would float away along with the butterflies in her belly.

They separated, breathless from the kiss, and Lakshmi hadn't ever thought she would swoon from a kiss. She closed her eyes to stop the dizziness, grateful she was in Yòuké's safe hands. But he took the liberty of placing another kiss on her lips, further disrupting the direction of her thoughts. She still kept her eyes closed long after they had separated.

"I think we have an audience, madam," Yòuké whispered into her ears.

Her eyes fluttered open, and she laid her head on Yòuké's chest. She inhaled his masculine scent, and Yòuké took a conscious step back. He chuckled nervously and said, "I'm sorry, I must smell like a pig."

"Yes," Lakshmi teased. "You do. But I quite like pigs. They're smart."

They dissolved into chuckles, and Yòuké pulled her into his arms again.

"I've wanted to do that since the first day I saw you," Yòuké mumbled into her hair.

CHAPTER 8   286

A delicious shiver snaked down her spine "On the Jezebel?"

"Yes."

"Well, I would have run away screaming."

Yòuké laughed. "Why?"

"Well, I wouldn't have known what to do with the rumblings of thunder, lightning flashes in my head, and the fluttering in my stomach."

"Oh, I see."

She heard the smile in his voice, and she pinched him lightly. "No one told me such a lowly servant had an ego the size of ten merchant ships."

"You've never met this sort of lowly servant, madam," Yòuké drawled, and Lakshmi giggled.

Her heart swelled with love for this man fate had brought back into her life. And she felt his love for her too, a delightful feeling like an invisible blanket around the both of them.

"I need to freshen up, Lakshmi," Yòuké said after a while. "We have a lot to do today. It's why I had to go take care of business."

CHAPTER 8   287

Lakshmi stared up at him, trying to figure out his plan. The mischief in Yòuké's eyes excited her greatly. She wondered how he had gotten the captain to dock for so long.

"I thought we had seen all there was to see, Yòuké," Lakshmi said.

Yòuké laughed. "You can never see all there is to Africa, darling. That's why we're going into the jungle today."

"The jungle?"

Excitement warred with concern in Lakshmi's head. "Is that safe, Yòuké? Aren't there lions and tigers and bears?"

"There are no bears in Africa, darling," said Yòuké, grinning. "Tigers, too. Maybe we'll see a Lion or two. Don't worry," he said when he saw her features tighten with concern. "I'm a native, remember?"

Lakshmi giggled. "How does that stop the Lion from eating us?"

"How about we find out?"

The trip into the jungle had not even begun,

CHAPTER 8   288

and Lakshmi was terrified. She expected the worst no matter how much Yòuké tried to allay her fears. Her heart was in her throat, and she jumped at every sound that reached her ears.

"I don't think this is a great idea, Yòuké," Lakshmi said, eyeing the jungle boots that looked to be several sizes above hers.

Yòuké had gone through the trouble of procuring protective equipment for both. Khaki clothes and wide-brimmed hats with nets around them to prevent flies and other insects. And there were backpacks, too, filled to the brim with supplies and materials they might need.

"Relax, Lakshmi. What's the worst that could happen?"

"Don't say that! Now you've jinxed it."

They sat in a shack just at the mouth of the forest, and they had their protective clothes on. Lakshmi stared at the boots with distaste. They were clunky and looked heavy. She supposed she would have to wear them if she went into the forest with Yòuké.

CHAPTER 8 289

Yòuké chuckled and gave her a quick kiss on the lips. "No such thing as jinxing. Now, put your boots on, and we will go. Here, I'll help you."

He squatted and helped Lakshmi put on her boots, one foot after the other. Yòuké couldn't stop smiling and then did nothing to quell her concern. He tied up her shoes and asked her if they were too tight. Lakshmi gave a vague answer because she imagined losing track of Yòuké, getting lost in the jungle, and then becoming Tiger food. There were many tigers in India, and she knew how vicious they were. Yòuké had insisted that there were no tigers in Africa, but Lakshmi was sure there were things in the jungle more dangerous than tigers.

But Yòuké didn't seem to mind. He seemed more determined to go into the jungle with Lakshmi now than when he had broken the news to her.

He helped her with her backpack and put on his, and they made their way towards the hole in

CHAPTER 8   290

the forest, which was beginning to look to Lakshmi like the mouth and elongated throat of some great dragon from the stories.

A shiny machete appeared in Yòuké's hand as if by magic, calming Lakshmi's fears a bit. The deeper they went into the forest, the quieter it became; the only loud sound was the clash of Yòuké's machete as he made a way where the brushes were too dense. Lakshmi stayed as close to Yòuké as possible. Her fear of getting lost and left behind was still quite intense, not that Yòuké would deliberately leave her.

Yòuké turned around to look at her, and there was a wild grin on his face.

Lakshmi smiled. "You're enjoying this more than I am, Yòuké. You were not joking when you called yourself a native."

Yòuké chuckled and said, "I should have gotten you a machete too. You'd have had fun clearing a path with me."

That wasn't a bad idea. But Lakshmi wanted her machete for another reason entirely.

Yòuké had stopped walking the bushes, and they had somehow come upon a beaten path wide enough to walk side by side. Yòuké sheathed his machete, to Lakshmi's dismay, and took her gloved hand in his.

"Ah," he sighed. The forest had come alive again now that Yòuké wasn't making such a noise and chasing the wildlife away.

"Like I said, nothing to be afraid of," he assured Lakshmi.

Nothing terrible had happened so far, and

Lakshmi was beginning to appreciate the coolness and the wonder of the forest.

"Look," Yòuké whispered, "up there." He pointed with a gloved finger, and Lakshmi struggled to find what he showed her. Then she saw it. A bird's nest. And she could see the bird's beak poking out of the nest. It was bright yellow and curved.

"It's beautiful," Lakshmi whispered, concerned that her voice would carry and spook the bird.

"It is," Yòuké agreed with a smile.

CHAPTER 8   292

She could see that Yòuké loved the jungle, and she imagined that it was just one of the numerous places he loved. She began to wonder if it was a good idea for him to stay with her in India when he clearly was a wanderer. She wanted a family someday, like she had told him some time ago. And she wanted stability also. A family where both parents were present. How long would Yòuké stay with them until the wanderlust took hold of him and made him want to leave, even if for a while? It was something to think about and talk about with him. But not now when they were both enjoying the ambience of the forest.

As they walked along the jungle path, they could both hear the buzz of insects and the rustle of leaves in the breeze. The jungle was alive with sound, and the two of them soaked in the moment as they walked. Lakshmi was aware that a change had come over Yòuké, he had become more animated and excited, like a child that was hiding something but doing everything possible to make sure no one suspected them.

Suddenly, Yòuké stopped and pointed to a small clearing off the main path. "This is what I wanted to show you," he said with a smile.

Lakshmi followed him into the clearing and saw that he had set up a picnic area with a blanket, a basket of food, and a bottle of wine. It was under a makeshift shade like a small hut, with carpets on the floor and several comfortable pillows to match the blanket. Lakshmi looked at him with a look of delight on her face.

"How did you do this?" she asked, still slightly in awe.

Yòuké grinned. "I came across this several years ago and thought it would be the perfect place to relax. I had a friend up here who helped fix the place. This was what I had to do this morning after I had handled business."

Yòuké was always finding ways to thrill her and give her happiness. She didn't know if she would ever be able to reciprocate, and that was a

CHAPTER 8 294

significant concern for her.

"Thank you," she said, touched by the gesture.

She could perceive the fragrance she'd struggled to place earlier. There was a lamp on the floor by the corner of the hut, an almost fresh plant burnt in the middle, emitting a pleasant smell that Lakshmi couldn't get enough of.

"What is that?" she asked curiously.

"It's medicine, and it'll keep the bugs away while we're here."

Yòuké took off his backpack and helped her get hers off. Then, they spread the blanket and settled in for a romantic picnic, enjoying the sights and sounds of the jungle around them. The surprise had been perfect, and Lakshmi was so happy that Yòuké had planned it.

Lakshmi's sides were hurting when Yòuké suggested they head for the ship. Her cheeks were hurting too, and she was full to bursting. Yòuké had made her day again.

And now it was time to return to the ship.

CHAPTER 8 295

Lakshmi hated to leave this place Yòuké had so lovingly created for them. A safe space away from everyone else. They were nestled in each other's arms among the pillows and on the blanket and carpet that surprisingly made a soft bed for the both of them. Everything felt so right, even the forest sounds that had initially made Lakshmi wary. The sounds were a part of the beautiful memory now.

"Come on," Yòuké mumbled, "it's time to go."

But he made no move to let her go. Lakshmi began to chuckle, and Yòuké joined in a moment later.

"You have to let me get up first, sir."

"Oh, that is true. I shall, eventually."

"I hope you can see in the dark," Lakshmi teased, "because you're leading us out of here in the darkness if we don't get up now."

"Fine." Yòuké sighed and made a big show of letting Lakshmi out of his embrace.

"Uh, Yòuké? Are we taking all of it with us?" Lakshmi asked after she had looked at the picnic baskets and all the other things they had met there.

"No, don't fret. My friend will clean it up tonight."

"Oh, who's this friend of yours?"

"A local, you've met him once," Yòuké said, smiling brightly.

Lakshmi thought she knew who it was—the boatman who had taken them on a cruise.

They left the forest with their backpacks, and Yòuké returned his machete. The journey out of the jungle was much more accessible. They had to follow the path Yòuké had already cleared earlier. They were momentarily out of the forest, stood at the edge, and stared at it.

"We should name it," Yòuké said fondly. "A name that belongs to just the two of us."

"Does it have a name already?" Lakshmi asked.

"Yes, but in the native tongue. Not English."

Lakshmi wondered for a while. Nothing came to mind to name the forest. So she said the thing

that had been on her mind since she had seen
Yòuké's efforts at making her happy.

"Will you join me in my cabin, Yòuké?" she
asked softly.

Yòuké hesitated momentarily, unsure if it was
appropriate for him to enter Lakshmi's cabin.
But when he saw the sincerity in her eyes, he
knew she meant it in the most innocent ways. "I
would be honoured to join you in your cabin,"
he said, walking together towards the ship.

Lakshmi held his hands tightly and wondered
how she would broach the topic of Yòuké's
wanderlust and what it meant for their
relationship. She decided to say it the moment
they were in her cabin. That way, he would have
his say, and she would have hers.

They climbed aboard the ship and made their
way to Lakshmi's cabin. Yòuké took in the cosy
atmosphere, noting the bookshelves lined with
books, the oversized porthole window
overlooking the sea, and the plush bed in the
corner.

CHAPTER 8   298

"This is quite the cosy cabin," he remarked.

Lakshmi smiled.

"It's my little home away from home," she said, motioning for him to sit on the chair while she sat on the bed.

Yòuké sat down and stared longingly at her, and he saw the desire in her eyes, too. She was still innocent, no matter what she had been through. And for her to invite him up to her cabin was no easy feat. It revealed a vulnerability that told Yòuké that Lakshmi was opening herself to him. And he wouldn't take her for granted.

"What's going on, Lakshmi?"

She came closer and said to him, "I have a concern, Yòuké, and I wanted to ask you a few questions. These moments I have shared with you on this trip are some of the best moments of my life. And you know that I want to be with you. But... I have watched you, Yòuké. And I know that you love to travel and see the world. Wouldn't you mind that you might not be able

CHAPTER 8 299

to travel so much while you're with me in India? I need you to think deeply before you answer, Yòuké."

Lakshmi could see that her concern had touched something in him. He was deep in thought, and Lakshmi continued. "It's a question I feel you must answer before we move forward. What do you want, Yòuké?"

Lakshmi waited in the silence of her cabin and watched the man she loved think deeply about all she had said. She wanted nothing more but to say he wanted nothing else but to be with her. She tried to touch him, help him realize the right place for him was beside her. But it was a decision he had to make on his own. She thought her question would go unanswered, but Yòuké turned to her and said, "My deepest desire is to find somewhere I belong, Lakshmi. Maybe it's why I've never settled anywhere."

Lakshmi listened attentively as Yòuké bared his soul to her, and when he was finished speaking, she placed her hand on his.

CHAPTER 8 300

"I understand that feeling," she said, "but I think you've already found your place. It's not a place on a map, it's a place in your heart. And I think that place is right here, with me."

Yòuké's heart swelled with emotion, and he felt his connection with Lakshmi pulse with new light. The knowledge that they were best suited for each other was a thrilling thought. He took her hand in his, and they sat in silence for a moment, enjoying the peacefulness of the moment.

And then, in a bold move, Yòuké leaned in and kissed Lakshmi gently on the lips. She didn't pull away, and instead returned the kiss, their lips meeting with a tenderness and passion that neither had experienced before.

They pulled away from each other, their faces flushed, their hearts racing.

"What...does this mean?" Lakshmi asked, her voice quivering.

"I think it means that I have fallen in love with you, Lakshmi," Yòuké replied, staring into her eyes.

And I've fallen in love with you too, was what Lakshmi wanted to say, but the words got stuck in her throat. Instead, she placed a hand on Yòuké's stubbed cheek and pressed her lips to his, telling him that she loved him with everything in her and all her strength, even if she could not proclaim the words with her mouth.

But the damage had been done already. She felt him pull away reluctantly and stand up. Then he smiled and put a loose strand of hair behind her ear.

"I must go now," he whispered into the silence thick with unspoken things.

"But..."

Lakshmi wanted to protest, but Yòuké shook his head gently.

"What's wrong, Yòuké?"

"Nothing," he said. Then he reached into his breast pocket and pulled out a necklace of brown twine and green precious stones.

CHAPTER 8   302

"I bought this early today. I forgot to give you while we were in the forest. I thought it would match...well, the tone."

Lakshmi didn't even look at the necklace.

"You're not happy, Yòuké."

"I am," he said, standing up and walking to her table, gently placing the necklace on it. "I'll just leave this here."

And to Lakshmi's dismay, he reached for the shrivelled-up piece of paper she had tossed on the table mindlessly several days ago, and her heart dropped into her stomach.

She watched him unroll the note Todd had left for her after that fateful night, and she saw the moment Yòuké's mood changed, and he froze as though all the blood in his body had turned to ice. Lakshmi lost the ability to speak at that moment, and she clenched her fist and tried to think of a way to prevent the storm that she knew was coming.

Yòuké turned around wordlessly, and he wouldn't meet Lakshmi's gaze. He stood quietly for a long second. And it looked to Lakshmi like he was reading the note repeatedly. She took a step forward, and Yòuké lifted a finger that froze her in her tracks.

Then he rolled up the note neatly and placed it on Lakshmi's bed.

He still didn't look at her. But a shadow had come over his features, and no passion or love was emanating from him like before, and his voice was cold as the grave when he said, "You shouldn't leave personal messages lying around like that. Anyone could read it. Good night, Lakshmi."

Then he walked around her, opened the door gently, got out, and shut it wordlessly behind him.

Lakshmi's strength gave out, and she sagged to the floor and began to cry. First, she had chosen to remain silent when Yòuké professed his love for her. And then he had somehow found the note that Todd had written to her, which was as risqué as love notes went, and read it right in

CHAPTER 8   304

front of her after she had kissed him with all the passion she could muster.

She didn't know which feeling was worse, the embarrassment or the sense that she had injured Yòuké deeply by the simple act of not destroying that note. Why had she tossed it so carelessly when she knew the note's contents would paint her in a bad light if anyone who didn't know her well read it?

Hot tears poured from her eyes. And she felt such intense hatred for herself, Todd, and Yòuké. She climbed out of the khaki clothes she wore and climbed into bed, letting the anger burn deep in her until she could no longer feel the pain of Yòuké's dismissal.

What about all the memories they had made these past few weeks? Did he think she was a woman of easy virtue? Did he think she still thought about Todd as the day passed?

Lakshmi was sure that that wasn't the case. But a part of her understood how Yòuké would see it that way, especially since his proclamation had not gotten a reply. And the forsaken note...

She wept until she could no longer weep, and then she fell into an uneasy sleep that had her tossing all night long.

*****

Yòuké could not bring himself to speak to Lakshmi. He was still hurt and angry about the note, but he knew that he was being unfair to her. He knew she had not meant to hurt him, yet he could not shake the feeling of betrayal. It was as if a dark cloud had descended over him, and he could not see a way out. He kept having dreams about this...Todd. And he knew that all that had happened was all in the past. But so soon after he had told her he loved her and she had not said it back to him, he had accidentally come upon the note from her ex-lover she had chosen to keep around.

That had stung much more than he thought possible. So he spent his days in the ship's library, trying to lose himself in books. But no matter how hard he tried, his thoughts always

CHAPTER 8   306

returned to Lakshmi.

One day, as Yòuké was sitting in the library, he heard the sound of someone clearing their throat. He looked up and saw Lakshmi standing there, her eyes red and puffy as if she had been crying.

"Can we talk?" she asked, her voice barely above a whisper.

Yòuké wanted to say no, to send her away. But something in her eyes stopped him. He nodded, and she sat down next to him. For a long moment, neither of them spoke.

And then, finally, Lakshmi spoke. "I know you're angry at me," she said, "and I don't blame you. I know I made a mistake, and I'm sorry. I don't want to lose you. I love you and don't want to live without you."

Yòuké felt his anger melting away as he looked into Lakshmi's eyes.

"I love you, too," he said, his voice hoarse. "But I was hurt by what I found in your room."

Lakshmi nodded, tears rolling down her

cheeks. "I know," she said. "I want to explain, but it's complicated. Do you think you can listen without getting angry?"

Yòuké nodded and closed the book he was reading.

"I should have left that note in England, Yòuké. And I should have destroyed it the moment we became reacquainted. But I didn't think anything of it. I need you to believe me."

"Then why did you have it on your table?" He had to know to ensure she wasn't pining after a man she'd left behind.

"I...I don't know!" Lakshmi was almost crying. "Surely you don't think I read it in my sleeping and waking hours?"

Yòuké's silence was all the answer she needed. She lost her temper then and stood up angrily. "I can't believe you would think so little of me, Yòuké."

All he did was stare at her with a blank gaze. Then they realized others were in the library, and Lakshmi stormed out.

CHAPTER 8   308

Yòuké sighed and laid his head on the book. He was so confused about the next step to take. And he didn't want to make the wrong decision. What did she expect him to think? It took him a while to realize that Lakshmi had told him she loved him. But it had been in the heat of anger. That was a comforting thought, at least. All he had to do now was get past the fact that she had kept Todd's note.

He raised his head and flipped the book open angrily, wishing that Todd was on the ship so he could have strong words with the man.

*****

It had been a week since Yòuké and Lakshmi's conversation in the library, and they had not spoken since. Those who had gotten accustomed to seeing the both of them together knew that they were having a lover's tiff, a huge one. They held themselves off from conversions around the dinner table. And there was nowhere else to go because the ship left the docks on the eve of their spat. So they spent their days avoiding one another. But they were as aware of each other as two souls could be.

Yòuké had not yet shaken off his anger at the man called Todd. He had realized that that was the actual cause of his anger. And it prevented him from reconciling with Lakshmi.

She had tried to approach him several times, but he had always turned away, unable to face her. And Yòuké found himself missing her despite his anger. But he did not know how to bridge the gap between them. And so, the days passed, each one a little colder and lonelier than the last.

Lakshmi was miserable, even when she was told by one of the crew mates that they would soon reach the port that would lead Lakshmi home. All she thought about was Yòuké. And he was right within reach. She could tell when he came on deck simply by how her body reacted whenever he was near. And she could tell that he was looking at her, too. She missed Yòuké's company, his warmth, and his laughter. And she

CHAPTER 8 310

knew that he must be feeling the same way.

One evening, as Lakshmi lay in her bed, she heard a light tapping on her door. She got up and opened it, and there stood Yòuké.

He looked down at his feet, not meeting her eyes. "Can we talk?" he asked.

Lakshmi's heart soared. She felt a little spark of hope, held onto it, and nursed it gently. She nodded and invited him into the cabin.

They sat down, and Yòuké began to speak.

"I'm sorry for the way I've been acting," he said.

"I know you must have had your reasons for keeping that note."

Lakshmi looked at him, surprised by his words.

"I didn't mean to upset you," she said. "I just didn't know how to explain the whole situation. But there's nothing I want to do with Todd. I promise you, Yòuké."

Yòuké nodded and grinned. "I figured that out when you said you loved me. And I understand.

CHAPTER 8 311

I'm sorry for overreacting. I just want us to be able to talk about things. I don't want there to be any secrets between us."

Yòuké came closer and pulled Lakshmi into his lap, then he nuzzled her neck and whispered into her ear, "No more secrets, Lakshmi."

Lakshmi smiled and wrapped her hands around his neck. "There won't be, I promise," she said.

They both felt a sense of relief and sat in companionable silence for a few moments, just basking in the knowledge that all was well with them again.

Then Lakshmi leaned back and whispered to Yòuké, "Have I told you that I love you, sir?"

"Yes, but tell me one more time."

"I love you, Yòuké."

"And I love you, Lakshmi."

All seemed to be alright with the both of them. But a question hid in the deep recesses of their minds. Especially on Yòuké's. His time away from Lakshmi hadn't all been spent pining after her and wishing they were together. He had taken a moment to ask himself personal questions along the lines of those Lakshmi had asked him that night. And truly, he hadn't been able to come up with answers to some of the questions. He knew he was the one who had asked to go with Lakshmi to India. But he had to be honest with himself first of all and with Lakshmi too.

He loved her with all his life, and he also loved travelling and his profession. Was there a way to balance these things he loved so dearly?

Was there a middle point where he could give himself totally to the dream life he had envisaged with Lakshmi and satisfy the adventurous spirit he had nursed all his adult life? He was at a crossroads. It was a dilemma that dulled the happiness he felt on those days when he stood with Lakshmi with his arms around her as they watched the sunset far on the horizon.

And it didn't go unnoticed by Lakshmi. She held him close one evening while they lounged in his cabin and she asked him, "I know there's something on your mind, Yòuké. Care to share what is?"

Yòuké pondered about the wisdom of revealing his concerns to her. It would seem very much like he was going back on his word, or as if he had changed his mind about wanting to be in Lakshmi's life. But that was not the case at all. It was just that he couldn't escape the wave of panic that overcame him whenever the thought of staying in one place for too long occurred to him.

"Remember, no secrets," Lakshmi reminded him, holding his hands lightly. "Whatever it is. Just say it. We've come too far to let minor issues get in the way."

His cabin suddenly felt too small to hold the both of them. So Yòuké got up and offered a hand to Lakshmi. "Let's go above deck, shall we?"

She took his hand eagerly and followed him up the stairs. The sky had grey clouds, even if the

CHAPTER 8   314

sun's rays spilt around them like a halo. Yòuké took that as a good sign. He was going to tell her how he felt, and then they would deal with the repercussions of his action afterwards.

"Lakshmi, you're the woman of my dreams," he started solemnly, putting every bit of emotion into his words. "And I want to spend the rest of my life with you..."

Lakshmi nodded, the love in her eyes shining as bright as the sun. She nodded and finished his statement, "But you think about it now and wonder if you wouldn't be living a life where you're restricted in some way. Isn't that right, darling?"

Yòuké sighed dejectedly and let go of her. "I'm so sorry if you're disappointed in me, Lakshmi," he said, not meeting her gaze. "I always panic whenever I think about it. And I don't know what to do."

Lakshmi wrapped her arms around him and pulled him into a long hug, holding him and letting him know that she understood exactly how he was feeling. She had him that way for a long time. They both knew that this was a challenge that seemed insurmountable. But Lakshmi thought in her mind that there must be a way to work around the bottleneck in the form of Yòuké's wanderlust. But now was not the time to worry about that. They would spend the time they had together as best as they could. Every other thing after that was irrelevant for now.

They pulled apart, and Yòuké held her face in his hands. He was in so much pain that it was a wonder how he was able to speak. He closed his eyes and prayed for strength. Then he said, "Another thing I have meant to tell you, Lakshmi. But I haven't had the courage till now. I'm getting off the ship at the next stop."

His statement was a dagger in her heart, and tears rose to her eyes and blurred her sight. There was no anger or hate in her heart for her beloved. All she felt for him was understanding and a boundless love she could not explain even

CHAPTER 8 316

if she tried to do so. The tears spilt down her face, but she gave a small smile.

"Well then, we make the best of our time. Don't you agree?"

"Why don't you hate me, Lakshmi?" Yòuké whispered in agony.

Lakshmi thought about his question for a while, and then she said, "Do you love me, Yòuké?"

"Yes," he answered, with all my heart.

"Then we'll find a way."

They embraced again and stayed that way until the cold winds drove them below deck and into each other's arms again.

On the day the ship was about to leave the port, a gloominess overcame Lakshmi so intensely that the other passengers avoided her like she was sick. And she, indeed, was ill. It was a sickness of the heart. She had spent all the time she could with Yòuké, and they had no more time together. And Yòuké had made no promises to her either that he would find her in

CHAPTER 8 317

Kerala or send word. It was easier that way or much harder. Lakshmi didn't know. But she was heartbroken, and so was Yòuké. He had held her the night before and sobbed like a boy again when he thought she was asleep. The dark circles under his eyes in the morning were the only indication that he did not sleep so well.

And so the time came for the ship to leave, and Lakshmi watched from aboard the vessel as Yòuké began to shrink the farther away they went from the port. She could feel the tears starting to form in her eyes. She wanted to run to Yòuké and beg him to stay, but she knew it wouldn't change anything. She felt a knot in her stomach as she watched him disappear among the crowd. The air around her grew colder, and she wrapped her arms around herself.

The sun was setting, and the sky was turning a deep shade of pink. Then, the last rays of sunlight faded, and Lakshmi felt the chill of the evening settle over her. She knew that she had to go below deck, but her feet felt like lead. She

CHAPTER 8   318

wanted to stay there forever, to hold on to the last few moments when Yòuké was still within reach. But eventually, she forced herself to walk away. As she made her way down the stairs, she tried to focus on her surroundings, on anything other than the ache in her heart. But no matter how hard she tried, she couldn't escape the pain.

She felt a wave of despair wash over her. She had hoped that they could find a way to make it work, but his desire to travel seemed stronger than his desire to be with her. And yet, as much as it hurt to let him go, she knew that she had to. She would always love him, but she had to accept that maybe they were not meant to be together. And if they were, then he would find his way to her. And so, with a heavy heart, and teary eyes, she made her way to her cabin, went inside and shut the door softly.

Even while she lay in her bed, the tears continued to fall, soaking the pillow beneath her head. She closed her eyes, but sleep eluded her. All she could see was Yòuké's face, his smile, his laugh. She could still feel the warmth of his hand in hers, the way his eyes had lit up when he spoke of the adventures they could have together even in such a place as Kerala. He had asked her if she wanted to follow him instead, travel the world with him. But Lakshmi had refused. She had had enough of the world. She wanted to go home to her family. But now, it was all just a memory. She felt empty, like a part of her had been ripped away. She didn't know how she would ever fill the void that Yòuké had left behind.

As the hours passed, Lakshmi's sobs eventually faded, and she was left with a numb exhaustion. She felt as though her tears had cleansed her, washing away the pain, leaving only a hollow shell. She drifted into a fitful sleep, dreaming of Yòuké, the sound of his laughter, and how he had looked at her with such tenderness and affection. But then, she woke up with a start in the late hours of the day and the harsh reality of his absence crashed

CHAPTER 8   320

down on her once again. She managed to dine with the others but her black mood shut down every conversation anyone initiated.

She realized a few days later that Kerala was no longer far. And she would have to move on without Yòuké. She prepared for her arrival in Kerala and she tried to put on a brave face. She tried to convince herself that she was strong enough to go on without Yòuké, that she could be happy without him. She told herself that he was only a part of her life, a moment in time that had passed. But deep down, she knew that it was not true. He had left a lasting mark on her heart, and she would never be the same. But she resolved to face the future with courage and hope, even if her heart was still broken.

Then a few days later, the ship pulled into the harbour at Kochi, and Lakshmi could see the shoreline crowded with people.

The air was filled with the scent of spices and the sounds of voices calling out in Malayalam. As she stepped onto the dock, she was enveloped in the warmth and chaos of her home country. But as she looked out at the crowd, she did not see any familiar faces. She had been away for so long. And she walked forward to her box, feeling completely lost in the place she had called home a long time ago. And she realized that she was dressed as an English woman, and it was a strange sight to see someone who was clearly Indian dressed in the garments of the English. She sighed and withheld a sob, wondering how she was going to get by. Then she felt a curious gaze on her and a young Indian man approached her warily.

She stared at him intently, noting that it was a familiar face. Then she realized in a flash who it was, and she vaulted from her perch on her box and threw her hands around the man's neck, squealing, "Vinay!"

Her nephew, Vinay, worked as a cargo carrier on the docks.

"Aunt Lakshmi!" he shouted, a broad smile on his face. "I knew it was you! You have changed

CHAPTER 8   322

Then he did a slow perusal and frowned. "How come you're dressed in this manner? Don't tell me you've forgotten where you came from?"

Lakshmi was too happy to respond. The joy of hearing her language being spoken was almost too much to bear. She hugged her nephew again and held on even as tears rolled down her face.

"Are you okay, Aunt Lakshmi?" her nephew asked softly.

"Yes, it's so good to see you. Look how big you've become!" she exclaimed. "I can't believe it!"

They broke into laughter and Vinay took her box and lugged it after them, launching into several stories at once of what Lakshmi had missed while she was away. Even while she listened to Vinay's stories, her mind began to wander. She thought of Yòuké, of the time they had spent together, of the way he had made her feel. But then, she forced herself to focus on the present and the family she was about to reunite

CHAPTER 8 323

with.

And she wondered what she was going to say when she finally saw her parents, her sister, and her nephews and nieces. Would all her thoughts of Yòuké fade away? Would the emptiness she felt be hastily filled by the joy of being surrounded by the people who would love her no matter what?

That remained to be seen, she thought.

Vinay procured a truck pulled by a donkey and they were making for the family house a moment later, Lakshmi seated up front with her nephew who was now a grown man. She felt a bit of trepidation as she anticipated her family's reaction. If Vinay had noted her limp he didn't say anything. But her mother and father would know. They knew what had happened to her in England, maybe the little Lord Michael had told them. And Meena. She had missed her little sister so much.

"We're here," Vinay said, beaming brightly. He helped her down from the truck and went

CHAPTER 8   324

around the donkey to pull her box.

Lakshmi adjusted the shawl Vinay had bought for her as they went past a market. She looked around in awe at her surroundings, noting how much everything had changed. Then an elderly woman with a bright red shawl stepped out of the door in front of Lakshmi and she froze when her eyes connected with Lakshmi's.

"Amma?" Lakshmi croaked.

Then everything was a blur as she embraced her crying mother and then her father came next and then the rest of her family trooped out endlessly from that small door her mother had come out of. The family gathered around Lakshmi, hugging her and welcoming her home. They told her about all that had happened while she was away, about births and deaths, marriages and separations, new jobs and new homes. They offered her food and drink, and they made her feel like she had never been away. And as the sun set over the horizon, they all sat together, talking and laughing, the past forgotten and the future bright. And Lakshmi knew that she was home at last.

*****

Lakshmi and her sister Meena sat arm in arm on the family house's roof, looking out over the city spread before them like a map. Meena's growth had shocked her the most. She was the same age Lakshmi had been when Lord Michael had taken her to England. But Meena was nothing like Lakshmi had been at that age. Her dark eyes were wise and knowing, and Lakshmi had wondered how much her parents had told her sister. Then Meena managed to get Lakshmi alone and told her all she knew, and the story had spilt out of Lakshmi like a leaky tap. She was a weeping mess when she was done. And Meena was crying along with her.

Then she started to speak about Yòuké and couldn't talk anymore. The pain was still too fresh. Lakshmi looked into her sister's eyes and saw understanding and compassion.

"You can tell me anything," Meena said,

CHAPTER 8   326

taking Lakshmi's hand in hers.

"I know, Meena," Lakshmi said, smiling. "You've grown so much."

Meena rolled her eyes, "Tell that to our parents. They seem to think I'm still a child."

"You are still a child, Meena," Lakshmi said sadly. "And I don't want you to ever experience what happened to me. Even with Yòuké."

"Tell me about him," Meena asked softly.

Where could she start from? When she had met him that first time in the belly of the Jezebel? Or when she had met him again as a different person on another ship?

And so, Lakshmi began to tell her about Yòuké, how he had come into her life and changed everything, and how she had felt when she saw him on the dock as her ship sailed away. The pain was indescribable. Lakshmi wanted to fold into herself and sleep for as long as she could until the memory of what could have been with Yòuké stopped hurting so much. Instead, she held Meena's hand tightly and took comfort in the strong and secure love her family had for her.

When she was done, she wiped her eyes and leaned into the chair. She took several deep breaths to steady herself, letting the wind dry the tears on her cheeks.

"I know it's silly," she said, her voice shaking.

"But I can't stop thinking about him."

Meena smiled. "It's not silly at all," she said. "It's human. And you love him. If it is meant to be, then you will both find your way to each other someday."

"Do you truly think so?" Lakshmi asked, failing to keep the hope in her voice from slipping out.

"Yes," Meena said with an assurance that was baffling to Lakshmi. But she held on to Meena's words as they watched the sunset and its indigo rays spill out all over the city beneath them.

*****

Years later...

Lakshmi hummed a lively tune as she ran a rag

CHAPTER 8   328

on the table. She had just finished chopping ingredients for a healing salve she was making and the scent of the herbs transported her to a different time and a different place. She had been very young then, and her sole purpose had been to care for a darling old woman called Lady Michelle. That had been the upside of that period of her life, the other things were steeped in darkness, up until that moment when she'd left the cursed place and the cursed family.

She smiled sadly as the memories came one after the other, some very bitter as to leave a sour taste in her mouth, and the others were so sweet that she basked in them, letting them stretch out until she could do so no more.

Her smile broadened when she heard a familiar whistle coming from somewhere behind the house. Pleasure filled her heart and she stopped her cleaning and cocked her ears to hear the whistling better. This was no memory, she thought fondly. This was her reality. She had found joy again, a thing that had eluded her sometime after she had returned to Kerala a couple of years ago. And then the impossible had happened.

She had found love again. For the third time.

She had come out of the barn after feeding the goats, and there he was, standing in front of her house like a wraith. And he looked thinner, as though he hadn't been sleeping well. Then she called his name and he twirled around and gaped when he saw her.

Then he had called her name so sweetly and tears blurred her vision even as she flew towards him like an arrow shot from a bow. She slammed into him and held on to him for dear life, calling his name again and again as if she wasn't convinced he was right in her arms.

Yòuké was in Kerala, right in front of her father's house, with dust on his boots and tears streaming down his face.

"I can't believe you're here," she whispered into his ear.

"Best believe, darling," he had said to her.

CHAPTER 8   330

"And I'm not going away this time." He had kept his word so far.

Returning to the present, she heard him shuffle into the house and she hid behind the door and waited for him to step into the kitchen. Then she reached for him gently and wrapped her arms around his waist.

"We have to be quick," Yòuké whispered, "my wife would be back soon. She's mean and you'll not stand a chance in a fight. Ouch!"

They broke into loud laughter and Yòuké turned around and pulled Lakshmi into a fierce hug.

"Hello, my darling," he murmured, kissing her all over her face and her neck. "I missed you so much today."

Lakshmi struggled to speak in between giggles. "You say that all the time."

"Yes, but I mean it every time I say it."

"Oh, in that case..."

Yòuké had a facility at the docks, a large building where he did his business of trading. It was the perfect balance. He was still close to the sea and the life he had not wanted to get away from, and he got to go home to the love of his life at the end of the day. He had chosen to go after Lakshmi some months after he had watched her leave on the ship. His life had lost meaning and he had struggled to find out what was missing. And like a blind man who had suddenly regained sight, he had discovered the reason for his misery.

The love of his life was in a small town in India and he was on a blasted ship heading to a place he didn't want to be. He had gotten off at the closest port and made his way towards his Lakshmi.

Lakshmi stared up at him lovingly, wondering how lucky she had become. Yòuké had come back to her three times. She wanted to float into the sky with happiness any time she thought about it.

"I have to go now, darling," said Lakshmi, "the girls would be waiting for me."

CHAPTER 8   332

"Right, the girls. I suppose I would have to make my own dinner."

Lakshmi chuckled, "Yòuké, you jester."

She lowered a tray of cakes from the counter and Yòuké's eyes bulged.

"And this is one of the many reasons why I love you," Yòuké said, reaching for a piece of cake and stuffing it in his mouth.

Lakshmi was a teacher in a school in the middle of the city. She taught girls proper control of the English language and courtly manners. They were girls from families that wanted so much for their daughters to go to England to further their studies or for some other reason. Lakshmi made it a duty to teach the girls other things besides the English language.

She taught them how to stand up for themselves no matter where they were, and how to separate truth from lies, and she taught them values and the need to always speak the truth no matter what. And above all, she taught them the

CHAPTER 8 333

importance of family, and the knowledge that love triumphed over the direst situations.

OPPOSITE PAGE

JUST SOME OF MY
BOOKS THAT ARE
AVAILABLE
ON AMAZON
SEARCH
DAVID DOWSON

CHAPTER 8   334

CHAPTER 8   335

Printed in Great Britain
by Amazon